BLACK BOOK

DYLAN JONES

PROLOGUE

I think it's best if I start by telling you about the day I met the Devil outside a saloon in Nebraska. I stepped out of the musty drinking hole, my eyes adjusting to the white midday sky. I clipped my watch shut and dropped it back inside my jacket.

Cupping a splintered match in my hands, I lit up another smoke. I had a three day shadow on my face and I was exhausted. Still sober though, and that was a start for now. I squinted down the high street, left then right. Not a soul. I shivered. My hand fell to my side out of habit and rested on my gun. Across the street, above the store, a shutter slammed shut. There was a time when I'd have done the same. Back when I was just another ordinary man, before I knew the truth of the world. I patted my left chest pocket, felt the bulge and clink of bullets. Comforting. Not as comforting as two pockets full, but there was no more time. There was no fanfare, no cloud of dust, and no clap of thunder. When I first met the Devil himself he was just sitting on the saloon porch behind me. Been there all along I guess, watching me check my gun and ammo. If he saw me flinch at all he was polite enough not to show it. And isn't that just a hoot?

'Marvelous day for a matrimony. Wouldn't you say chief?' He wore a white fitted tuxedo, and dabbed at his moist forehead with a black silken rag.

I grimaced at the sound of his voice. It wasn't raspy or evil like you'd expect, and the tone was pleasant enough, but it was *wrong* all the way to the end of the dial.

'Pearse Slake. Delighted to meet you.' He snaked out a long thin hand, and I noticed yellow dirty nails, tuxedo or not. When Old Handsome spoke for the second time I had cleared the fog enough to at least answer him. Incredible how quickly we can adapt.

'You may have the wrong impression of me even before we start.' I said calmly. There was no way in hell that I would voluntarily shake that hand. He didn't pause even for a second, and his hand was back in his lap as if it had never left. A town sheriff back in those days had very little in the way of perks, but refusing to shake the hand of a stranger was one of them, and thank the good Lord for that. I looked away and over the dusty horizon for a merciful couple of seconds. Anything but those eyes.

'Apologies for the unannounced intrusion chief, but I come seeking only a little water for myself and perhaps a bed for the evening. Then I shall get on with my business.' His skin rippled as he spoke.

'As I said, you may have me mistaken for someone else. I'll be polite right back to you, and there's no harm in that. But I'm not your friend stranger, and you certainly aren't welcome here.'

For a moment I thought he would end it right there. Just cut the pretense, string me up, and try and make me drink my own wine. But he stood up quietly, quite the gentleman, adjusted his hat, and gave me a wink.

'Nevertheless , it has been my pleasure to finally meet you Chief.' and with that he walked away, smiling.

My head throbbed. I stood my ground until he was well over the rise and out of sight and then I sat down hard onto the wooden stoop.

'Jesus wept.' I exhaled hoarsely, beads of sweat drew icy fingers down my back. I dabbed a shirt sleeve onto my forehead and it came away darker. I felt the nausea almost pass, but before I knew it, I had spilled my breakfast all over my boots. My head pounded as if nails had been driven through it, and at that moment I would have killed a man for his whisky.

When I was eight years old I spent the summer at old uncle Ned's farm in Ohio. He called me to the sty one morning and asked me to help him lift out one of the pigs. I could see one of its hind legs had been gnawed down to the bone by something, *another stronger pig maybe, or a wild dog*, he didn't know. What he did know, he winked at me, was that we were going to eat well that week. Being eight years old and a man of the world, I knew full well what good old uncle Ned meant to do, and my stomach dropped down a few floors.

Nevertheless, we hauled the doomed pig to the yard, and strung him up by his hind legs. (Maybe if I had ever learned to call a pig *it* instead of *he* , I wouldn't have baulked so badly at what was coming.) Anyway, when Ned carved up that poor pig's throat he bled out quietly, without any of that squealing they do. What he did do however was feverishly lick up that pool of blood that was gushing out of him. He did that right until the end came. I guess it could be that pigs will simply eat when they're hungry, and he didn't know enough to worry that it was his own blood. But in my heart I knew he was trying to keep that blood inside himself where it belonged.

When I heard the Devil talk to me, that's what came to my mind. That desperate strung up animal, clutching at the very last chance of life. The damned, lapping up its own blood.

You may think that I imagined a strange man to be something that he wasn't. I only wish it were so. There's no doubt as to who he was because I have met him many times since.

Besides, on that dark day in Nebraska, what the Devil didn't know was that it was I and not he who had orchestrated our little meeting, and had planned it for well over a year at that.I had read many reports describing evil aftershocks following visits from the devil. Countless witness testimonials in many different languages over hundreds of years. People from vastly different cultures and geographical and chronological locations recounted similar stories of unspeakable horror. Suicidal pet dogs running into white-hot fireplaces, babies gouging their own eyes out. They all began the same way; A well dressed stranger crossing their paths. A polite man with a scratchy, scaly voice and filthy yellow claws.

For me, the aftershocks began with a distant rumble. I brushed the slick strip of hair from my brow and winced past the sunlight toward the horizon. I could see no thunderclouds, but on heaving myself up, I could see a cloud of a different kind. Dust approaching from the West. Maybe seven men on horseback, coming at us like the wind.

As if in reaction to this train of thought a woman's scream pierced through the saloon doors behind me. *That didn't sound too good.* I pushed briskly through the doors and stepped into the gloom, turning my back for a moment on the approaching omen.

My eyes took a second to focus, and the first thing I saw in the gloom was the quick butt of a rifle. I flinched and dropped down half a second too late, and caught the worst of it above the bridge of my nose. I didn't feel a thing but a bright white star flashed in front of my eyes. I landed hard on my side and the sawdust floor tried to envelop me in darkness.

'Are you one of them?' the silhouetted man's spittle stank of bad whisky. He'd used his Winchester as a crutch and was leaning heavily on it to get real close. He was close enough to kiss me. Kiss me or kill me. I wasn't in the mood for either. I brought my left hand defensively up toward the gash on my forehead. The movement of a man in shock, checking his injuries. It's a universal gesture and is the total opposite of threatening. Which is why he neither expected or saw my other hand shooting palm out, punching his rifle out from under him. It popped out of place, and he fell hard, face first onto my chest. Still blinded by the bright flashbulbs in my head and the contrasting darkness of the room, I grabbed for his nape with my left. I wrenched a thick fistful of long greasy hair and spun him round on his back like a snared fish. Before he even had the voice to complain I crashed my right hand down on his larynx, hard. He howled and squealed, his hands clawing at his throat. I pushed his face into the dirt and got up onto my feet.

'One of who?' I growled at him, thumbing back on my revolver. A thin line of blood snaked into my left eye, giving the world a terrible red hue. I must have looked like hell, because the woman screamed again. My eyes almost got their act together and I could make out five other faces apart from the loon on the floor.

A woman of pleasure, her dress torn at the neck, was cowering behind the stair bannister. She had a palm shaped mark on her face that was still throbbing a bright red. A sleepy old man who looked around a hundred and eight peered at me over wire frame spectacles. In his gnarled hands he had two dusty black aces and two black eights. Not a bad hand. Shame he'd never get to play them. His gambling partner, a young boy no older than twenty, had pissed in his boots and was desperately trying to avoid any eye contact. By the bar, a large Ox of a man was twisted around and grinning at me, still sipping his whisky. He wore a long grey coat and had a faceful of whiskers beneath the muddy brim of his hat. His huge frame was making his wooden stool screech every time he moved. One of the stool's legs had already splintered. Years of humid saloon air had maybe started it, this big Ox had finished it off.

The empty glass and empty seat beside his own told me he was the lunatic's drinking pal. Behind him, with the bar between them, the barkeep was staring at me intently. Not as old as the full-house holder, but getting there steadily. He had one eye shut tightly and his other was blinking down a long Remington rifle barrel, which was pointed straight at my head.

I spat blood and tried my best to ignore the gun. With any luck, the old timer would miss if he got excited enough to shoot. Besides, I needed an answer from the coughing idiot on the floor.

'I'll ask again,' I nudged him in the ribs with my boot, 'and since there's a big cloud of hooves headed this way right now, I suggest you be quick in finding your tongue.'

He let out a long rasping cough. 'Fudging broke my throat!' he wailed thinly. 'You're one of 'em. You've come here to fudge my shit up. He tole me you were coming. He fudging tole...' The rest was lost as he rasped into another coughing fit.

A quick glance at the Ox at the bar, his eyes gleaming, his tongue feverishly licking his top lip over an imperceptible smile, told me that it was *he* who had set the loon off like a crazy firecracker. Question was why?

The Ox was dressed like a man passing through. He had a traveling coat, well-worn but expensive boots, the beard of someone who slept under the stars and the deep color of a man who walked often or far during the afternoon heat. In contrast the guy on the floor was a local drunk. No shoes to his name. No money to be spending in the saloon. I had seen him before a couple of times, roaming the outskirts when the traders passed through. But I hadn't seen the Ox before. They seemed like an odd couple to be sharing a drink and a conversation. Time to shake things up.

I threw my gun casually to the Ox, 'Shoot him.' I said, as I took a stride toward the bar. The Ox didn't disappoint. With lightning quick reflexes, he had caught the revolver and reversed it at my head just as I reached the bar. I poured myself a large drink, ignoring the two guns now pointed at me.

The bar tender had taken a cautious step back and was alternating his line of fire like a pendulum. Me, the Ox, Me, the Ox, tick, tock, tick, tock. I couldn't reach the old man's rifle with the bar in the way.

Not without a prop.

Tick, tock, tick ...

I swung the bottle of Jack in an arc. Tock; It smashed squarely against the tip of the barrel as it pointed toward the Ox. The bottle evaporated into fragments, knocking the rifle-butt into the old barman's eye socket and he yelped back, dropping the heavy gun on the bar. The woman squealed and ran, aiming to hide behind the old card player. She slipped in the boy's puddle and went sprawling into the table. I felt more than heard the hollow noise her head made as it clipped the corner. The card game was well and truly over, as woman, table, drinks and cards all crashed to earth in a pile.

The boy scampered away to the back room, clutching his wet drawers as he went. The old man simply blinked in disbelief, like a solitary house left untouched in a tornado's wake. He threw his aces and eights - *Dead man's hand* - after the rest of the pack.

The Ox and I got the best deal and were drenched in fine American whisky. The Ox barely blinked. I swiped the heavy rifle off the wet bar.

'I wouldn't do anything rash.' The Ox's slick drawl matched his agility, not his size. I looked down and saw that he had invested the split second distraction in advancing his gun hand. His finger was tensed on the trigger and the muzzle was sticking well into my gut. I gave him one last chance.

'We're all friends here big bear. I had to make sure old Fred here didn't hurt himself with this old blunderbuss.' I grinned at him to show how friendly I was. He grinned right back, and pulled the trigger.

When a man pulls a trigger at point blank, he's not expecting to have to be on his guard afterwards. At worst he's thinking he should be ready to pull the trigger once more toward the guy's friends. But it took that Ox maybe only a second and a half to pull that trigger three times at point blank.

What's the only sure-fire way to know if a man with a gun intends to kill you? Easiest way is to give him a gun, before he pulls his own. That way, at least you know where the bullets are.

It took me half a second to raise the old Winchester up to shoulder level. I used the other second to pummel the heavy end into the Ox's face. It hit him like a steam train. I heard something crack. Yet he barely flinched. His eyes were on fire, and he meant to kill me with his bare hands. It didn't matter. His flinch had made him lift his leg off the floor for a moment, putting all of his weight on the stool. I pistoned my leg out and snapped the seat's bad leg clean in two. Then two things happened at once.

The Ox fell backwards like a felled tree, crashing heavily onto his back, and rapping his head solidly on the bar's boot rail. At the same instant the saloon doors splintered open and three large men on heavy horses stomped in. Steam rose from the horse backs and black-red blood streaked down their flanks from gored spur marks.

The whore awoke at the noise and screamed again. The wail didn't last as long this time. There was a loud bark from the doorway, and the girl's head disappeared in a puff of red. Her lifeless body toppled to the ground and bled. Blue smoke rose from the shotgun barrel of the horseman closest to the bar.

No one moved. Even the loon stopped his whinging and locked his eyes on the new arrivals. A fly ambled along the bar, quietly enjoying the warm whisky. I wondered where the rest of the posse had gone. I glanced behind me at the back-room door. Pissing boy had opened it a notch and was gawping through the crack.

'You.' The eldest, a lean wiry man with pockmarked skin, pointed at the bar man. 'Three of your finest water pans for your horse guests, and a taste of scotch each for their riders.'

The old guy looked to me for help, didn't get any, shrugged, and went about serving the drinks. I noticed that the dead girl's hand was lying in the puddle of urine. For some reason, that made me even angrier than the fact that she no longer had her head.

I cleared my throat. 'Seems we may have outdone ourselves with the introductions. This young girl now lying headless in piss water was Coraline.' I spoke to their front man. 'She's pleased to meet you. And you are?'

Three simultaneous gunshots rang out. The boy was shot in the head through the back door, the lunatic screamed in pain, and the old guy with the cards mewled like a sick cat.

'Anything else to add, Sheriff?' A shotgun and two large handguns pointed towards me, still smoking. I risked a quick glance across the room. The Ox still snored softly on the floor and the barman was frozen mid-pour. The old card player died in his chair, a dark rose blooming on his shirt.

A scream pierced the silence. 'They shot me! I tole you they was comin'! I fuggin' tole you!' The lunatic's screeches were cut short by three further shots. He flopped along on his belly, his long wild hair splayed into a dark fan in the sawdust, then was still. It seemed the shotgun shooter also had a handgun.

'Now, you only have two more of your flock to protect in here shepherd, so I suggest you speak only when spoken to. Wouldn't you agree?'

I said nothing.

He dropped gracefully off his horse and slapped its rump. The horse trotted to the far corner of the bar, where the barman had filled three cooking pots of varying sizes with almost drinkable water. The horse drank gladly. The two other riders followed, and the horses joined their thirsty companion.

'We're looking for a man, Sheriff,' I assumed he was the leader, or that his two gruff looking companions were mute. He grabbed his whisky off the bar and breathed in the aroma, his eyes shut. 'and we think you can help us find him.' He handed the other two whiskies back to his co-riders, the shot glasses like thimbles in their bear hands. They made the Ox on the floor look like a rag doll.

The leader looked at me in amusement. 'You've been spoken to. Hence, you may speak.' He smiled, almost politely.

'You already know I won't help you. Which makes me wonder why you haven't shot me yet.'

The wiry man laughed, a real hearty laughter from his belly. 'Oh, that's *beyond* good. Maybe I won't kill you now because I'm impressed with your *rapport*. Is that the plan?'

I shrugged. I hadn't meant anything clever by it. I was just buying time. Try to work out what this clown really wanted, and who for. Before I killed him.

'See this tall gentleman here? Step forward Jake. Thatta' boy.' He put a hand on the shotgun fellow's arm as he stepped toward him. He couldn't quite reach his shoulder and keep it natural looking. 'How long have we known each other Jake?' he asked shotgun. *Jake* grinned at him, and with the onset of his smile I realized Jake was barely a man. He was a boy in a man's body. A farm hand maybe, working hard all his life, his body grown way before his years. His face weathered more than usual by time spent outdoors.

'Since forever I guess.' His voice cracked and I noticed the resemblance in their faces. Not father and son, but close enough. Perhaps uncle and nephew, cattle owner and cow-hand.

'That's right son,' he turned his smile to me, 'show the nice Sheriff what I bought you for your sixteenth this year.'

Christ, only sixteen.

Jake produced a bone handled blade from his belt and held it up proudly. Now the act of a big man all but dissipated as he showed off his prize possession. 'It's for skinning rabbits and such.' he blurted. 'It's...' he stopped suddenly, realizing too late that he was forgetting his place. He blushed a dark crimson and handed the knife to his boss, who twirled the knife in his hand as he spoke.

'You see Mr Sheriff, I'm a man of many qualities. But unfortunately for you, sentiment isn't one of them.' I saw a flash of silver as he moved to slap Jake in the face. There was no noise and for a moment I thought he'd missed. Then a terrible gurgling noise came from Jake, and red froth bubbled from his throat. Jake smiled and tried to cough. It was such a clean cut he didn't even know it had happened yet. It dawned on him slowly and he clamped both hands over his leaking throat.

'Please..' he whispered to me as he fell to his knees. I stepped toward him, already taking off my jacket ready to put pressure on the wound.

'Ahem...' The wiry man stepped nimbly between me and the boy, and gently pressed the tip of the knife through my buckskins and I felt the cool blade scratch my groin. 'He's done. Leave him be. Besides, the little prick's been helping himself to my whores. And I hate to share, don't you?' he winked at me, and I saw for the first time that his eyes were almost colorless.

The other big guy had apparently seen worse than this and actually chuckled. He seemed older, and a little darker skinned. He clicked his tongue twice and the horses harrumphed and trotted toward him. He led them quietly out of the Saloon. Leaving me alone with the maniac, the old barman, a snoring Ox, and a dying sixteen year old boy, bubbling quietly from the neck. Mercifully he had either fainted or slipped into his final moments, for he lay on the ground silently, his lifeblood quickly draining from him.

The maniac shut his eyes and rubbed his temple with his thumb and forefinger, as if all the killing had given him one hell of a headache.

'Now then Sheriff.. or do I call you...' he waited for me to fill in the blank. I didn't.

I saw the old timer behind the bar reach slowly for the rifle. I made eye contact and shook my head fractionally, *No*. He seemed thankful for the intervention and sagged as he exhaled, as if his neck were no longer able to hold the weight of his head.

The maniac with the knife opened his eyes and looked into mine. 'I guess it's just plain old 'Sheriff' then.' and smiled. The voices of a group of men shouting and whooping somewhere out in the street followed by screams of women reminded me that I had seen seven men in the distance, and not three. I hoped they weren't all as slippery as this character. I only had one pocket-full of bullets after all.

One of the men, a good-sized, sweating man, barged in through the busted saloon doors. He seemed about ready to shit his pantyhose.

'Sir, you just *got* to come see!' his face was red and he was wearing a big shit-eating grin.

The maniac calmly turned around and cracked a bullet right through the man's teeth. The guy still looked delighted even as he crashed to the floor, the back of his head a gaping, bloody hole.

'You just can't seem to get them these days.' the maniac said calmly, as if we were discussing it over breakfast. He misread the blank look on my face as a question and continued. 'The damned workers. Always forgetting the big picture. Always beating on some damned bitch or stealing some god-damned animals. Lord damn it!' This last he spat out with the first real hint of any feeling I'd seen from him yet.

He flipped the knife over in his hand and threw it down in anger. It spiked and juddered into the floorboard near the sleeping Ox's head, missing his right ear by a couple inches.

'After you good sir.' He motioned me toward the sunlight now streaming in through the splintered doors, waving me forward with the still-smoking gun. 'Let's see what these dumb-wits have gotten me into now shall we?'

Three men were dragging a heavily pregnant woman through the dirt. A man lay on the floor in their wake, blood trickling from a gash across his temple. The girl's husband I presumed. She was kicking and fighting like a cougar. One had her by the hair, one was pulling hard on her clothes, and the other was laughing and kicking her bare legs as she went. I saw that this third had his hand down his trousers, and was feverishly trying to undo his belt.

Enough was enough. Time to get rid of these maggots.

I jolted forward a step as if I was making a dash toward them, then stamped my foot down hard and reversed direction and heaved backwards with all I had, hurling my right elbow viciously backward, swinging it past my shoulder at about a hundred miles an hour. The maniac was fast enough to react to the dash forward with a leap after me, but if he noticed the double back he left it a fraction of a second too late. He leapt face first and my elbow caved in the front of his skull. There was a terrible crunching noise and his body went limp instantly. He fell like a dead dog, his face a mask of red. I picked up his gun and aimed it at the trio. They smiled at me. Like they were having so much fun they couldn't switch to business mode quite quickly enough. I smiled back.

The pregnant lady screamed, a high wailing whine.

I fired four shots. The first blew a black hole where trouser monkey had been exploring himself. I could see red daylight through his thigh. The second bullet took off the right half of hair-puller's face. Except for his eye. It dangled in the wind. He stayed alive for maybe half a second to enjoy it. The third bullet went through coat-tugger's left lung, and a spray of arterial blood arced over the whole party. The fourth was for the big horse guy now standing a foot behind me, his finger tight on the trigger, maybe a second away from blowing my head off with his shotgun.

I dropped to my knees and spun at the same time. I fired the shot before I hit the ground. He looked stunned. He had the shotgun in one hand, his revolver in the other. He looked at each hand in disgust, like he was more disappointed with himself than he was about the fact that his guts were trailing behind him like fat pink spaghetti. He aimed his pistol at me and then died on his feet. His carcass crumpled in a heap in the dirt.

A slow clapping echoed through the windy street. I instinctively aimed at the noise and blinked the grit from my eyes. The Ox was on his feet after all it seemed. Maybe sixty yards away, leaning on the saloon's porch. His nose was broken where I'd hit him with the gun.

'Most impressive Sheriff Jack. Certainly a lot quicker than you were indoors. Must take you a while to get warmed up.'

I saw it then. Not a party of seven men. But eight. One sent out ahead to scout quietly. The others to follow on afterwards, big and loud and ugly. The Ox had been playing me all along. If he was expecting a conversation he was going to be disappointed.

I ran through the scenarios available. Didn't like my options. I had fired four shots from the gun, the maniac had fired two before that. Empty. I let it drop to the floor.

Adrenaline is good for two things. Flight and fight. I put everything I had into flight. *Towards* the Ox. I closed 50 of the 60 yard gap quickly. My lungs burned and my leg muscles bunched into tight coils. I pistoned my arms to gain momentum. I felt like I could run through walls. The Ox remained where he was. He sneered, his lips peeling back, his teeth almost canine in the sunlight. I was almost on him, and his hands were still resting on his hips. Relaxed almost. Something was wrong. If he had a gun, he would be aiming it by now. No reason not to. The sun glinted off his buckle and I suddenly remembered. The boy's knife as it pronged the ground near the Ox's face. The Ox meant to skewer me. And I was doing all the work for him. I was running toward that knife as fast as I could. Too late to stop now. Three yards to go. I watched his eyes. A man could bluff in hundreds of ways but the eyes couldn't. I was almost on top of him when they changed. They seemed to go darker a fraction of a second before his right hand came up, the blade a quick flash in the light.

When a man drops to the ground or slows himself down, it's always predictable where he'll be at the end of the movement. Unless he doesn't even know himself. I kicked my left leg hard up to the right like I was kicking a rabid dog and let the momentum spin me around and down. I was going to fall hard but I was also moving quickly away from my expected tangent. The move had an unpredictable outcome because I wasn't limiting myself to the known safety positions of a man in a controlled fall. I was spinning all the while, yet falling toward him. The blade scratched my sleeve as it sliced past. Just where my belly had been two fractions sooner. And then I was crashing into him at full force. I saw the knife jerk out of his hand with the impact. Then his chin hit my head, my head hit the ground and we were a tangle of limbs and boots and dust and rocks.

Even as we rolled, I felt his sledgehammer blows on my back, on my neck, on my chest. He had fists like cannon balls. If one of those connected with my face, I wouldn't be getting up again. I couldn't even see him, let alone hit him. The world was still upside down and a spinning blur. Purple lights danced across my field of view. I opened my eyes wide, and looked for the brightest light. Two more blows, one to the shoulder another to the chest. I was running out of time. His next combination was likely to kill me.

Then I saw what I was looking for. When a man looks directly at the sun two things happen automatically. First, his eyes clamp shut, and second, the image is burned onto the retina. The world was no longer a sea of incoherent images. It was now a blank bright red canvas with a single perfect white disk shape toward my right shoulder. I knew exactly where I was at that frozen split second; facing eastward, directly away from the saloon.

I hauled myself toward where I thought the timber platform ended and launched off into empty space. I fell two long feet and landed hard on my side in the dirt, the air knocked out of me. I heard the Ox breathing heavily, scrambling after his prey. I rolled back toward the wooden overhang and slotted neatly under the saloon porch. I figured the Ox was an intelligent man. He would work out within three seconds that he couldn't squeeze in after me and would instead head toward the easier option of the shotgun by the door. Then it would be another two seconds to pick up the gun and another four to reach under the floor and blast his way into the gap after me. Seven precious seconds.

I thrust two fingers into my left boot, took out the folded rag in there. Inside it was a single translucent capsule, filled with black liquid. As the Ox stomped loudly toward his gun, I bit down hard on the vial. My vision blurred and the last thing I heard as the darkness came was the Ox's voice as he peered into the gloom.

'Just like shooting cats in a crate.' And he pulled the trigger.

I didn't hear the gunshot. Or feel any lead. I was already a thousand miles away, 3 days further in time.

ONE

An ice-cold gale whipped California's shoreline. Night was fast approaching and only a single gull braved the winds. The bird ventured a little deeper out to sea, skimming the swelling waves, waiting for her chance to take a bite. A dark shape appeared in the depths below her, much bigger than the swell's usual inhabitants. It rose quickly toward the surface, and the gull squawked in protest, letting the wind carry her away to more uneventful waters.

The shape crashed out of the waves, thrashing its arms to stay afloat. As the wind lashed at its face, its naked bipedal form shuddered and retched, emptying its stomach of salt water. Its muscles shivered and spasmed in the cold as it fought to stay above the surface. It looked around in the fading light and saw infinite blackness ahead toward the horizon, and only a faint smudge of something in the opposite direction. Its survival instinct opted for the latter, and it kicked and dragged its way towards the shore.

The animal did not consciously know what it was, or how to exist, but instinctively it swam.

The darkness was complete by the time the exhausted creature dragged itself onto the sand. The moon dominated the sky and the animal stared up in awe. It examined itself, curious of the world in which it had just arrived.

A memory flash. The creature cowered in defense, mistaking the memory for reality.

Another; Faces. Humans. Violence. He looked at his hands. He was human. He could think. He saw a big bear snarling at him. The bear's nose was bleeding. The bear opened its jaws wide and lunged at him...

Sheriff Jack jolted awake, drenched in sweat, still lying where he'd lost consciousness at the water's edge. The sky was a dark red now. Nearly daylight. He sprang up, and screamed in pain as the electricity speared his brain.

He was hit by a second attack, and burrowed his face in the sand in agony. His vision was a white hot blur and his gums bled. Pummeling the sand with his fist to focus the pain, he tried to remember the meditation techniques. Bullshit. They never worked. The only reason anyone time-travelled more than once was because they never remembered that it felt like dying.

The bear-man... The Ox. His memories were still swiss cheesed, but Jack's fog slowly cleared in short bursts. He dragged himself up, fighting against the ice-cold finger piercing his skull. He walked like a drunk on a ship, away from the open space, toward the safety of the cliffs. The sun was almost up and he needed to find shelter before he lost consciousness again.

His dreams were fragmented. Violent. He jerked awake with the low sun on his face. He could hear voices and instinctively pressed himself down against the cool stone of the cave. Through gaps in the foliage outside he could make out four men, Indians, looking for something. Looking for him?

They wielded sharp tools and wore nothing but fur and leather. He held his breath and listened as their voices faded.

Jack ventured out through thick undergrowth, saw only their tracks and exhaled. He was at the foot of a great cliff. At the top he could see grass, but down here there was only sand and weeds. His mouth felt like sandpaper. He looked around for a way up to a better vantage point. Gripping the rocks with both hands, he scrambled up a gradual incline and found himself at the top of the lowest outcrop. There was nothing but ocean to the west. Rocks and trees to the east. North and south only offered more coastline. He started east. Water would be first. Then some clothing.

TWO

The huge steel doors rumbled open and two silhouettes walked in from the hangar bay. One was a slim young brunette in a serious grey suit. The other was a tall African-American male in his late thirties. He scanned the entire area methodically as he walked. A security team fell in behind and covered all the exits points. Warm air and the drone of machinery wafted in after them.

A uniformed man on the wrong side of forty marched across the polished steel floor to greet them. 'Mr President! Welcome! How was the flight?' General Daniels smiled as he caught up to them, pumping the hand of his old friend without breaking stride. He nodded a smile to the attaché as the heavy doors rumbled closed in the distance. She blinked, and smiled back.

'You should know better by now, General.' President Benjamin Freeman stood a few inches taller and a few pounds lighter than the General. 'I would much rather have walked here, had we the luxury.'

The General laughed out loud. 'You always were our best man on the ground, Ben.'

'Let's walk and talk Jim. Any further news?' The President's long strides had the other two working hard to catch up. The General steered them toward an entrance hatch. 'Only from this end sir, there have been no further signals from our Alpha. We have Beta juiced up and ready to drop in on the source signal as we speak. If we hurry we'll be just in time for the show.' The President stopped. 'An extraction? That's fantastic. So why aren't we celebrating?'

'It's not that simple quite yet. Through here please. Mind your head.' They ducked into a long service tunnel that snaked deeper into the compound.

The long corridor eventually opened out into a small reception area, with large vacuum-sealed glass doors on each wall. A single potted shrub by the central desk only managed to magnify the sterility of the place. A man of about thirty looked up from his terminal as they entered. The CRT's glow coloured his face an artificial green.

He snapped to attention as he realised who had just entered. 'Please check your tags here sir, ma'am... and, Mr. President.'

The brunette removed her magnetic badge and swiped it across the terminal's camera. It bleeped and her badge lit-up green. She replaced it on her jacket. 'Sir, if there's nothing else, I have some clearance documents I need to go through for the return flight.' nodding toward the smaller door. In the room beyond, banks of white shirted office workers went about their day.

'Sure, thanks Cal. I'll see you at the de-brief.' He smiled and turned his attention back to the General.

Daniels waited until Caroline's long legs were through the door and it had hissed shut behind her before speaking. 'You still hauling that old data recorder around with you Ben? Christ! She's probably logging everything you say.'

'She's actually much quicker than most of the new ones. Besides, the company insisted. The public love synthetics. Hell, she's probably worth forty percent of my votes by now.'

'Shit, it seems we've come a long way since the wars. People are too damned quick to forgive.'

'Not everyone it seems.' The President smiled. He swiped his own badge. It flashed amber and buzzed. The President looked puzzled and tried again. Red light. The receptionist looked flustered. The General seemed unshaken.

'It's okay folks. Just a simple security measure. High ranking officials need double-clearance to pass through the doors from here on in. Prevents any kidnap attempts. You'd thank me if you were being dragged through at gunpoint by some nut job right now.'

The receptionist flinched a little.

The General spoke into his badge, pressing the pad of his thumb against the outside as he did so. 'Double-clearance required for primary entrance. General Jim Daniels requesting.'

A female voice, electronic, spoke over the room's speakers. 'General Daniels, recognition confirmed.'

A few seconds passed and an older bespectacled face appeared at the door, making visual contact. He spoke into his badge, his voice amplified through the room's speakers. 'Double Clearance response. Lieutenant Adams responding.'

Again, the same female voice. 'Lieutenant Seymour Adams recognition confirmed. Guest to confirm within 10, 9, 8...'

'Swipe your card please Mr President, or we'll have a damned Swat Team on their way here in just under 6 seconds.'

The President looked bemused and swiped his card. It blipped and turned green. The door unlocked with a hiss of warm air. General Daniels ushered the President through into the dark corridor, before following him in. Lieutenant Adams stood to attention as they passed, then sealed the entrance behind them. The reception area went back to its calm air-conditioned normality. The receptionist blinked and tried to remember what he had been doing earlier.

'So where exactly are you stopping the bad guys from taking me?' The President grinned as they walked through the maze of dark brushed steel and black rubber. Warm yellow pin lights followed their progress through the corridors.

'Not *where* Benjamin, but *when*.'

The President shuddered as he considered the possibilities; A whole new breed of terrorism.

They arrived at another set of large plate glass double doors. The General swiped his card then requested double clearance for the President. A short man in a lab coat confirmed the clearance from inside the locked room, and the female computer started her monotone countdown again. The President swiped his card quickly this time, turning it green. As the doors slid open, the President looked thoughtful.

'How do you decide who's a high enough risk to warrant additional security?'

'Well, we run a series of algorithms. Each iD card as you know is personal to the individual, so it's just a matter of deciding who's at risk. With you, it's easy. Top priority. No question. Then we have various diplomats, royalty, even celebrity names crop up on the protected list. Aside from that it's an automatic green light for all official personnel and their vetted guests. Then it's back to red light for the regular folk. We want to keep them out for different reasons of course.' The General grabbed an electronic clipboard from the wall and signed in with his thumbprint.

President Freeman scanned the area, and saw people milling about with a hushed urgency. 'Simple but effective solution I suppose. Can't it be compromised?'

'Not easily. They'd need someone with access to walk them in and an accomplice to confirm clearance on the inside. And we screen our personnel from birth. We know more about them than their own mothers.'

They walked into a long, bright room. Lined against the furthest wall were glass tubular booths, like upright sleeping pods. Maybe ten in all. Banks of electronic lights and cables hummed quietly between them. The pods were all empty, except one. In the nearest were two men. Both strapped in at the midriff, facing outward through the glass, back to back, with only a sliver of plate glass between them. They were naked, clean-shaven and greased with what looked like petroleum jelly. Electrodes linked their heads and chests. One of the men looked to be of native American descent. His eyes were closed and he was breathing regularly. His chest muscles spasmed intermittently as he meditated. The other was a bear of a man. He stood almost a foot taller than his companion, and his viking-like frame filled his half of the pod. He breathed rapidly, his chest rising and falling quickly. He was huge. The President thought he looked bigger than any soldier he'd ever worked with. He looked more like an Ox.

'Mr President. Meet our Beta Soldier.'

'Which one?'

'Both.'

The President raised an eyebrow.

'This stuff isn't throwaway like we had during the wars Ben. Plus, as you know, The Company doesn't have deep pockets these days. No spoils of war to keep us constantly funded. Cost exceeds a billion per pod per launch, if it works or not. We have to minimize the risk of errors any way we can.'

'Two Betas, in case one wastes your money by not surviving?'

'There's a little more to it, but essentially... yes.'

The President whistled softly, 'I'm glad I got out when I did. That doesn't exactly boost morale. Why stop at two? Doesn't it make sense to launch four, five, ten guys?'

The General smiled. The President still had the same dry humour. 'Believe me, we've considered all the options Ben, and two is just fine. After that, it gets too expensive to house them during the launch.'

The President shook his head in awe. It had been years since he'd been anywhere near a time pod. He massaged his upper arm from habit, calming a phantom pain that had long gone. 'Stats?'

General Daniels studied his notes, 'Nano cells enable them to use 67% of their muscle power instead of the usual 20%. Night Vis brain patches as standard; Infra red and UV. Synthesised blood cells allow 58% increase in oxygen concentration. Big Red here can lift close to four times his own weight, stay underwater for 7 minutes at maximum exertion or see a man blink three miles away in the dead of night.'

'Impressive. And the little guy?' He nodded toward the Native American

'Those *were* the little guy's stats. His real name's Wolf. Big Red to his buddies. Never call him that to his face. Anyway, no stats for the big guy. File's classified. Fast tracked from The Company's special ops. Apparently the best there is.'

The President studied the soldier. Through the thick glass, the Ox's chest looked like a slab of armour plating. A small oriental man with snow white hair scurried past and flipped a selection of intricate switches on the Ox's side of the pod.

'We'll be ready to initiate their launch in a few minutes Ben. Want to settle in for the ride?' the General motioned to a separate viewing area staged a little higher within the room.

As the President made his way up the gantry stairs, the two-storey steel wall behind the pods buzzed down, revealing a secondary glass wall to be the only thing between them and the vacuum outside. The President's breath caught in his throat as he saw the view. Millions of stars pricked a black sky, and looming large and centre, a thousand miles away, the dying planet Earth.

He'd seen pictures of course, and holographs, but never like this. The wars truly had been brutal. He released a breath he hadn't even realised he was holding. Outside, a smooth piece of debris the size of a football floated upward past the window, bumped gently against the glass and resumed its path into deeper space.

The President dropped himself into a leather chair as the station rumbled on its ever-constant orbit. No one knew whose side had struck Earth's final blow. Some said a hole had been drilled far into the Earth's core by the synthetics, and a thorium bomb released inside. Others thought it was a targeted surface blast from the American lunar estate. Whatever the cause, the effect had been devastating. It had ended the wars, but at the greatest possible cost. The millions who weren't killed had to be relocated to already overpopulated colonies.

A third of the Earth's spherical area now floated in fragments above its orbit. The planet looked like an apple core just after a firecracker had been detonated inside. At ground zero, the surface mantel had evaporated as if it were nothing, and the molten core had exploded far out into space, cooling into a perfect freeze-frame of the atrocity.

The President forced his attention back to the mission. He watched the General suggest a few last minute adjustments, saw the familiar restrained excitement in the personnel's faces. They were close now; He remembered the electric atmosphere all too well.

Inside the pod, the Ox's breathing calmed to match his co-pilot's, and the President watched him close his eyes as he prepared himself for the countdown.

THREE

The dog was a mongrel. Jack was sure of that. The damned thing could smell him. He was sure of that too. Jack crouched behind the thick roots of a tall old oak. Two miles east were some primitive wooden structures, an outhouse and a dog on a long rope. The dog was barking, looking straight toward him. Couldn't see this far maybe, but his nose seemed to work just fine. No one had paid any attention to the animal yet. But they soon would. There was a fresh water stream about halfway between them. It cut directly in between him and the dog. There was no way to skirt around to it either. No trees, no rocks. He'd be totally exposed if he went any further. Unless he wanted to crawl through the grass for miles like a god-damned snake he was going to have to shut that dog up somehow. He was already feeling nauseous. He had to get hydrated soon or he'd be in trouble.

'Where are your trousers?' The boy, six, maybe seven, had been in the tree above him all along. So much for years of recon training.

'Who taught you to sneak up on people like that? Get down here boy. Quietly.' Jack kept his voice low. The wind had carried his smell to the dog, it would surely carry their voices too.

The boy giggled and climbed down. His poncho snagged firmly on the last branch and the boy yelped in panic, his neck suddenly pulled upwards by his own weight against the rag, his feet kicking only air.

Jack sprang up, hoisted the boy out of the overcoat and put him down safely on the grass. Somewhere in the distance the dog stopped barking. The lad wiped a tear from his eye and shrugged off his calamity. Jack grabbed the Poncho off the tree and tore the neck line a little more.

'Hey! You can't do that mister, that's mine.' The boy's fists were already tight balls of fury.

'Calm yourself son. I'm only borrowing it,' Jack stepped into the poncho like a woman would her skirt, 'Besides, if it weren't for me, you'd likely have no neck left to put it around. So quit your hollering.' Jack winked, and the kid seemed satisfied with that and sat down quietly.

Jack felt ridiculous in the garb but suddenly a lot less vulnerable. 'Now tell me, was that your dog hollering over there boy?'

'That's Barkuss. He barks.' The boy smiled, his straw hair and toothless grin sending a shiver down Jack's spine. A memory? Already gone. It happened a lot these days.

'Who lives with you and Barkuss? Is your Pa home?'

The boy shook his head resolutely, 'And I don't have no Ma either, so you can save your askin.'

Jack knelt beside the boy, 'Who feeds you and your dog son? Who looks out for you?'

'The man does.'

'Which man?'

'That'll be me, sonny.' A sturdy looking old timer stepped out from behind the tree. He was aiming a rifle directly at Jack's head, and his hands weren't wavering. 'What's your opinion on that?'

FOUR

The President watched the pods all light up, one by one, even the empty ones. A low, unpleasant noise filled the chamber. Like scratching steel rods across ceramic. Tubes that snaked into the pods stiffened as they filled with black liquid. The General busied himself with two main data monitors. He signalled a tech over. Pointed at some figures. The tech shrugged. The President couldn't hear anything over the howl of machinery now, but lip-read well enough to get the idea. Something wasn't right. Nothing major judging by their reactions. No one shouted, no one ran, no machines were powered down. The extraction was still going ahead. Maybe just some calibration issues. The Ox opened his eyes and smiled at him. The President smiled back politely. Wolf was still motionless.

As he glanced over the machines again, President Freeman felt uneasy. He swiped a thumb across his brow, and it came away wet. Just the anticipation and the electrical humidity perhaps? He didn't think so.

He had survived years of intense warfare by following one simple rule. Always follow your gut instinct. During training for the Elite they'd been trained ruthlessly. He remembered the burning cabin test. Only one entry point. Possible hostage situation. His superior barking at him to get in there. Screaming in his face. The hostages would all be dead if he didn't go immediately. They were going to fail him if he refused. He had followed his gut. He had ignored the Major, commandeered his truck, and rammed it through the hut's wall.

Inside were six drone synthetics, heavily armed. No hostages. The surprise attack allowed him to take four out before he even got out of the truck. The other two he killed with his hands.

Out of a hundred and thirty eight soldiers, he was the first of only three men that made it through to Elite squadron that year. General Jim Daniels had been the second. Their missing Alpha Soldier Jack had been the last. The three of them had become brothers over the years. Had survived together. Never lost a fight. Never left a man behind. Until now.

This last thought triggered more alarm bells in his head. He tried to immediately calm himself. Used the same trick they had been taught before time-jumps. Increase distance from yourself. Look at yourself within the room as others see you. Imagine yourself in the pod. He had always found that part hard because they had never actually seen the inside of the pods. They were always... Christ! His thoughts crashed down on him at once. They were always asleep in the pod. To eliminate any chance of sabotage. The Ox was awake!

'Jim!' The President launched off the gantry and sprinted toward General Daniels. The noise was too loud. The General remained hunched over a keyboard with a superior officer. They scratched their heads and pointed at data streams. An Asian technician looked up idly from her paperwork and stared curiously at the vip running towards the General. At the same time, a door opened behind her and Cal walked in, her long legs swishing through the gap in the lab coat. The President had just enough time to wonder why Cal was wearing a lab coat when the technician's face disintegrated. Her lifeless body slumped forward and Cal stepped over her, her handgun still smoking a thin blue wisp.

'No!' The President suddenly understood. In that split second his mind pieced together multiple key events. He was trained to react to unplanned scenarios proactively. Never question why. Just win. Survive first, ask why tomorrow. He flipped a steel coffee table up in front of him and ran with it, toward the Synth. Not Cal anymore. Just another Synthetic. She was the first priority. Eliminate the primary threat, then abort the mission and eliminate the other sleeper cell; The Ox.

The machines howled ever louder but finally the General had heard the commotion. He turned around and saw all hell breaking loose behind him; The President being shot at. The President swinging the solid steel table at Cal's head as she reloaded. A puff of blood on impact. Her head knocked to an unnatural angle. The General vaulted over the desk and put three bullets from his own sidearm in the cyborg's skull.

The President didn't even pause. He sprinted toward the pods.

The General saw the Ox pound the toughened glass between himself and Wolf, who was still in a deep sleep. The glass splintered under the force. Ben was still half a room away.

The General aimed directly at The President's back. 'Ben! Lunar Base!'

The President didn't respond. Damn! Had he even heard?

The General pulled back on the firing mechanism, breathed out and fired. Just as his finger tightened on the trigger and before his hand jerked back with recoil he saw the President tuck into a forward roll. Perfect. Years previously they had used the exact same manoeuvre to eliminate a bomber during a moon shuttle hijack.

The bullet whistled over the President's head and ruptured its target, the capsule's main supply pipe. Oxygen squealed out of the flayed rubber hose. Nothing happened to the power levels. The machines still rolled. Damn it. The auto-shut down hadn't kicked in. The President was already back on his feet and powering toward the Ox. There was no time left for finesse.

Brute force was all they had now. Still running at full pace, Ben swung his left arm as hard as he could toward the glass. The heavy table leg he held in it becoming a fierce club.

The thick glass only chipped, didn't even crack. The Ox's arm was through the inner partition, reaching deep into the twinned chamber. The President's mind raced through possible scenarios. It didn't make sense. The emergency manual controls were directly beneath the Ox, not behind him. The Ox's fist was bloodied, his knuckles shreds of skin from the huge blunt force trauma. The President took a heavy breath. Best bet was to pull him out, worry about details later. He switched to his right arm. Aimed for the glass's weak spot. Near the hinge. A huge blow. The table leg dented on impact but the pod remained intact. An inhuman moan made the President jerk back a step. Black-red fluid sprayed across the inside of the pod.

'Shit!'

Wolf thrashed around in his harness like a wet fish. He was cut deep across his right thigh. Arterial spray quickly filled the pod. The Ox had a makeshift blade in his hand fashioned from a shard of glass and was panting heavily. The inner wall lay in fragments. Blue sensor LED's lit up one after the other along the glass bottom where the blood pooled. A klaxon rang out. It sounded like it was coming from everywhere at once.

'Chance of a little help here?' Ben shouted. He put his whole weight against the pod. Used his good arm to lift the bottom. It weighed much more than he remembered. 'Fuck!'

'I'll shut the power cores down!' the General opened a floor panel. Started ripping out electrical couplers. Lights went out along the walls. But the pods remained active. Their self-contained lighting throwing a red glow across the room.

The President managed to tip the pod maybe another inch before his fingers slipped and it crashed back down. Its solid mass shaking the walls. Too heavy. The Ox alone probably weighed more than he could lift since the last surgery.

'It's too late Ben, the pods go into lock-down within seconds of detecting DNA contamination. They're powering themselves now.' The General held up the last of the detached power couplings.

'Damn it! How long have we got Jim?' President Freeman tried to focus on a clear strategy.

The General just stood gaping.

'General! I need our position right NOW! How long before this whole place is swarming with that Swat Team?'

'I don't... they're 3 minutes away from the furthest corners of the station. Optimum time for response. From here, a little less.' The General blinked at the bloody carnage unfolding only feet away from him, 'But they'll never stop him in time Ben, the pod bays will release automatically in half that time.'

'They aren't coming to stop him, General. They're coming to clean up after him.'

'What?'

'It's the Company Jim! We're both nothing but damned puppets. And they're on their way *right now* to cut our strings.'

Behind them, the Pod's hydraulics hissed. A motor noise almost like a shuttle's undercarriage whirred and clanked below deck, locking unseen struts into place. The pod jolted, then sank down quickly into its launch tunnel. As he was taken away the Ox looked the President right in the eye and saluted. He was backdropped by smeared red glass and the slumped Beta soldier Wolf, still in stasis, his life draining quickly.

The steel top of the pod became flush with the floor. The glass unit detached and a loud blast of air-loss as it was sucked out into open space. The General and the President watched through the hull's glass wall as the time pod's thrusters flared back up into their field of view in the distance. It made minute micro-adjustments to its trajectory, and powered onward on its pre-programmed course; Toward Earth.

FIVE

Jack looked down the steady barrel pointed right at him and raised his arms. Not out of fear. He had held none of that for a long time. But out of respect. The old man had just stumbled across a naked stranger on his land. The least Jack could do was let the man be angry.

'I'm only looking for water old man. Sorry about the intrusion.'

The old man's face cracked into a grin. He lowered his gun. 'Sir, you have no idea how long I've waited for those words. Oh my. Come here Jack and let these old eyes see you again.'

Jack dropped his arms and took a cautious step forward. 'I can't recall...'

The old man shifted his hat and blinked at Jack in the sunlight. Jack realised the man had tears in his eyes. He grabbed Jack by the shoulders and shook his head. 'My, my, my. A wonder. Yes sir, an absolute marvel.' The man beckoned the boy over. 'Take a good look at this man's face son. This is the face of a hero. A god-damned hero no less.'

The boy giggled and hid behind the old man's britches.

The old man wiped his eye then clapped his hands together. 'Well gentlemen. Now that we're all here, I guess we have some eating and drinking to do!' he gave his gun to Jack to carry and slapped him on the back. He hoisted the boy high in his arms and set off toward the house.

Jack was confused but glad of the warm welcome. His memory might come back to him later. In the meantime he could drink, rest and eat. Now that food had been mentioned he suddenly thought of nothing else. Jack set off after them. The boy was peeking over the old guy's shoulder, studying the new strange arrival.

The old man shouted without turning around, 'Oh and remember to watch your step!'

Jack's foot slid in something dark and he almost went tumbling. Horse manure. The boy giggled and clasped his hands over his mouth in delight.

The old man laughed, a big hearty laugh. 'Maybe you'll miss it next time.'

Jack thought maybe the old guy was crazy after all. In the distance the dog started barking again. Jack felt an odd comfort in that. Now that he was no longer an intruder, the dog's yelps made him feel at home.

SIX

The Ox exhaled. Finally clear of the station, he strapped himself in and de-activated the autopilot. The Ox saw the gargantuan vessel's plethora of blinking lights shrink to a singular point in the distance. The pod rocked him sideways as it corrected its course. Wolf moaned softly behind him. There wasn't much time. The Ox twisted around and tearing off his own emergency supply pipe, strapped a makeshift tourniquet around Wolf's upper leg. The cut was deeper than he had intended, but worse than it looked. It had been a fine balance between releasing enough blood to activate the lockdown, and not cutting so much that his comrade would bleed out. He examined the wound. It would heal itself. At worst, Wolf would find himself in an unknown timeframe because of the nano-fluid loss. Ox hadn't used his own blood because he couldn't risk changing his own dose. He checked his levels. They were a little high, but well within the safety parameters. He would very likely shoot back only a day or two past his target date. He flicked the thruster switch. The pod rocked and shuddered under the increased G-Force. They shot head first toward the remains of the late, great planet earth.

Small fragments of debris rattled against the glass. Then larger chunks, more often. The Ox craned his head round and saw nothing but planet. They were on the outskirts of the dwindling atmosphere. Now for the fun part.

The pod guided itself toward a vast piece of blue surface miles below, avoiding large pieces of asteroid as it went. It hurtled toward the ocean, at times flaring its rockets. But only left or right. Never to slow itself. The Ox watched the altimeter count down through the volatile clouds until they were a good mile above the surface, then the front thrusters blasted on and they slowed fractionally. The rocket flames dazzled the Ox's forward view and he turned his attention back into the pod. He kept his eye on the altitude and waited until it approached 500 meters. The lower he could get it, the better their chance of survival. Outside, a raging wind bucked and threw the falling capsule like a raft at sea. The Ox rapped his head on the glass. Wolf groaned with each jolt. The altimeter said 20 meters and hovered there.

Showtime.

Unstrapping himself and turning around to face Wolf, the Ox cut off the thrusters and counted the fall in his head. When he reached six he pulled Wolf's magnetic coil. Half of the pod sheared away and Wolf was sucked out into the howling winds.

'Safe jump kid.' He watched for a fraction of a second and saw Wolf 's dead weight evaporate into fine particles a couple of meters before hitting the fiery sea. Ox removed his own magnetic coil and felt the nano-cells in his bloodstream activate all at once. He was sucked out of the pod and had a sense of falling. The pod crashed heavily into the sea to his far right.

Then there was no sea.

There was nothing.

SEVEN

'Feeling more like yourself?' The old timer grinned at Jack over the broad wooden table.

Jack had eaten more than his fill and had washed it down with about a gallon of water. He felt like he could nap for a week. The old man had given him dry clothes that almost fit, and they had spent the rest of the daylight hours preparing then eating what little the bare cupboards had yielded. Jack saw that the boy had finally fallen asleep, his head heavy on Jack's shoulder. A single candle flickered on the table, making the urge to sleep that much stronger.

'Kid likes you. Seems you pass the test.' The old man winked. The dog, an ugly brute, nuzzled Jack's hand and wouldn't stop until Jack succumbed and scratched his head. The old man's smile faded. 'Go on now Barkuss. Off with you!' The dog hung its head low and lay down quietly under Jack's legs.

'He's a good dog, but we don't get too close to him. He's for working.' The dog blinked up at them, his head on his front paws. Outside, the crickets played their moonlight song.

'I can't stay old man. There are some bad people looking for me. You and the boy aren't safe while I'm here.'

'That much is true. But we'll be safe for long enough to say what needs to be said. You'll stay here tonight. Those damned injuns won't travel this far in by night. Then tomorrow there's someplace you have to see. The big fella ain't too far away neither and so we'll keep our wits about us nonetheless.'

'Care to tell me how you know so much about another man's business?' Jack found himself too tired to be anything but curious. For this man was indeed a curiosity.

'You're not the only man who knows a little about father time.' And with that he was on his feet. 'You can rest your eyes where you sit or take the dog's sack if he'll let you.'

He scooped the boy up and put him on a wooden crate in the corner of the room. He put his own overcoat over the boy then went to the door, his rifle in one hand, his smoke in the other.

Jack's eyes felt like lead weights. Maybe he could make some sense of this old man's ramblings in the morning. 'Where will you sleep?'

The old man turned as he opened the door, 'I won't need sleep tonight son. I'm dreaming with my eyes wide open!' and gave a high chuckle as he went out into the night.

Jack slept fitfully that night. His dreaming mind went back to a man in a white suit. The man grinned yellow snake teeth. He wasn't a man at all. The Devil himself pointed across the street at a face in an upstairs window. Jack saw his own lifeless face staring back down at him. Then the shutters slammed shut with a *bang!*

Jack opened his eyes and sat up straight. His shirt was soaked through. The candle had burned to nothing. He saw the boy fast asleep in the corner. The dog's ears were pricked up and he was looking at the door. Its eyes were alert and its fur stood on edge. The dog had heard it too. Jack shushed the dog's whining and slid behind the door. Another *crack!* A gunshot.

Jack crashed out through the door, the dog bounding after him. He almost fell over the old man who lay sprawled on the grass.

'What in the name of heck are you playing at?' The old timer was up like a rattlesnake. Jack saw he had a rabbit by his feet. Another lay twitching maybe twenty yards from them. His rifle smoked from the barrel. Jack exhaled. Seemed the old man had been catching their breakfast.

'Seeing as you're here now, I'm going to get me some shuteye. Remember how these work don't ya'?' he handed Jack a handful of rounds with the gun. 'If it moves, shoot it. And I ain't talking about rabbits here. We've got plenty of them, yes sir.' The old fellow smiled and squeezed Jack's shoulder as he went inside. Judging by the colour of the sky, Jack thought the old man could get a couple of hours sleep before sun-up.

Looked like it was his turn to keep watch. He crouched down low, his back to the house. The dog whimpered and sat next to him. His ears twitched as he sniffed the wind, keeping his own watch. Jack smiled to himself. He knew the dog could smell a man at over two miles. He hoped the old man was right and that he wouldn't have to. He was kind of curious about what the man needed to show him. He'd hate to have to leave before that happened.

EIGHT

The Ox rode west. He'd been moving west for a few days. Since he'd fired his gun point blank at a man and shot nothing but a ghost and the clothes on his back. But he knew where the man had gone. He knew exactly where to pick up the trail. He scratched his beard and wiped sweat from his brow. He'd already been stuck in this primitive hell hole for longer than planned. He'd landed a little earlier than the technicians had accounted for. A few months earlier than even he had expected. He'd had time to get his bearings. Made some new friends. Planned the ambush. It hadn't gone well but he never dwelled on failure. He lived by a simple rule. Always adapt immediately, find another way forward.

There was no way in hell he could have calculated where and when Jack had leaped to, even if he had seen the dosage volume. Different people absorbed the blockers differently.

But even so, he did know. He had seen the exact location marked on an electronic map that wouldn't exist for another 446 years. The blip they'd received. The reason the Ox had been sent here in the first place. The only marker Jack had flared up in over 12 months since he'd gone dark. The Ox had memorised it. Had sat up through the night before launch, burning it into his memory so that even after leaping, he wouldn't forget. He could still see the marker's glow in his mind. A slight deviation in the known values of space-time, pinged from the super-data bank and translated into simple schematics on their screens. A white beacon at the point of departure, a green one at the destination.

The Ox had quickly seen what the scientists hadn't. A singular blip of time travel after so long in hiding. It meant a man forced to jump. Perhaps thrown into a situation he hadn't dealt with in a long time. A man taken by surprise. The Ox guessed that no man from 1862 was a match for an Elite of Jack's calibre. But someone from his own time might be. Someone trained as an Elite certainly would be. Someone like the Ox. He had known then that it would be his own early arrival that would cause Jack's sharp exit, with his trail blazing through time and across their future screens like a big neon sign.

He gave the horse a nudge with his heels and felt its muscles powering harder underneath him. Far away on the horizon he could make out the western coastline, the late afternoon sun glistening off the waves. The Ox smiled and re-doubled his grip on the reins, and the horse thundered onwards.

NINE

Klaxons wailed through the space station's corridors. Far, far below, the Earth's scarred remains glinted in the sun's cool light.

In the main lab, President Ben Freeman had torn off his tie and was using it to stem blood loss from a male technician's arm. It was only a graze, but the guy was out cold. The President checked the man's pulse. Stable. Seemed he'd taken a heavy fall during the synthetic's attack. *The synthetic.* For four years he had called Cal a friend and a trusted colleague. Now she lay burnt out and smouldering on the deck, still clutching the pistol she had meant to kill him with. Hair and skin had burned away revealing the cold steel of her skull. The three neat bullet entry holes in its base charred and smoking. All around them, static crackled and damaged machines sparked in blue bursts. Red emergency lights flung long shadows across the floor. A few smoking electrical conduits added to the effect. General Jim Daniels ran back into the room clutching a rifle and manually closed the entry doors.

'What's the damage?' The President checked his watch as he spoke. Just over two minutes left.

'Levels three and four are clear. We have a lot of personnel down and wounded. Seemed your friend left a hell of a mess on the way in.'

'How long will these blast doors hold?'

'Not long enough. We have to leave. Now.' The General looked like a man on the edge. His old training was at last kicking in but the President could tell he was struggling to accept his new situation.

'Jim, we can't blast our way out with your old service rifle and two handguns. Those clear levels won't take us to a hangar and even those will be teeming with SWAT inside of 90 seconds.'

Jim's face darkened. He clenched the rifle tighter.

The President looked him in the eye. 'Jim. There's only one way out of here for us now. How close to Jack can you get us?'

'Christ, Ben!' The General's shoulders visibly sagged.

'How close?'

The General breathed in once then let it out sharply. 'I could get within a couple of years at best.' He turned away with new found determination toward the control panels, rebooting switches and powering up the pods.

'I can live with that.' The President stripped his shirt off and tied it around his upper arm. He kicked open a supply cabinet and grabbed a medi-kit. He took out a needle and feeder tube, flexed his forearm, found a vein and made the insertion. He took two ampules of the concentrated nano-fluid from the kit and fed them into the tube. He held the end of the tube above his head to speed the flow. He threw a kit to the General. 'Better get cracking Jim.'

The General's hands were a blur as he re-activated the pods. 'Just get in Ben, dammit. I'm right behind you.'

Behind a two-way mirror above the launch gallery, a young Asian man in a dark suit closed his eyes. He pinched the bridge of his nose as if willing away a headache. Behind him, in the darkness, a wheelchair whirred forward a few inches.

The man in the suit turned toward his boss and raised an eyebrow. The dark shape in the shadows nodded almost imperceptibly.

The suit clicked a button on his analogue watch and spoke into the device.

'Team B, green-light. Containment only. No casualties. Repeat, no casualties.'

Elsewhere, deep in the bowels of the space station, a double-height set of doors screeched open on their runners and a dozen men in black combat gear spilled out. Ahead of them the long maze of corridors snaked toward the launch facility. They moved quickly and carefully, rifles loaded, safeties off.

TEN

The night lingered on until finally it gave way to red hued clouds in the east and beads of wet grass underfoot. Jack stretched out a crick in his back and automatically patted his pockets for phantom smokes. He'd regained most of his lost memories throughout the night, and most of his cravings too by the looks of things. He could once again feel the whiskey demon gnawing at his brain, like a gargoyle perched on his shoulder. He shrugged it away for now. Moved his mind elsewhere.

He hadn't seen anything that spooked him after the old man had retired. A fox had caught him almost napping, but the dog had woken up the whole damned country with that little visit. Jack had tied the mutt to a post after that.

The hut's door squeaked open and the boy came running out barefoot. He fastened his britches as he ran, a big grin wedged on his face. Like a kid on Christmas morning.

'How does she find you this morning son?' Jack put on his sternest voice.

The boy frowned playfully, but fell into the part naturally enough. 'Fine and dandy so she does. Mister, did you kill all the injuns that snook up on us?'

Jack stifled a chuckle. 'Well son, I guess the last hundred or so got scared after I buried the first hundred, so'n they decided to hot-foot it over that hill instead.'

The boy looked mesmerised and tried his hardest to spot the last of the fictional Indians fleeing over the ridge.

The old man clattered a tin cup with his spoon outside the shack, and both Jack and the boy understood the timeless signal that breakfast was being served. The dog seemed to know it too, and he whimpered and whined on his hind legs to show it. Jack shooed the boy on and smiled to himself as he watched the kid dart through the long grass. That boy could run like a hare. Jack untied the dog, which thanked him by trying to chew off his boot.

'Go on! Get!' he swiped his hat at the dog, which bounced out of the way easily enough and contented himself instead with alternating bounces and orbits around Jack's legs, all the way to the house.

Jack ducked inside and was surprised at how much like home this modest dwelling already felt. Maybe all houses did, when the warm welcome inside promised such protection from the cold.

The old guy had laid out an ugly but wonderful smelling feast. Jack saw the remnants in the cooking pot still burning in the corner. The old man clanged a bowl down each for the three of them. 'This ought to keep you warmed up sir, but mind how she chews. Maybe one or two of them pellets still busy killin' these rabbits.' And with that he folded almost double and went into silent spasms. Jack's heart bumped up into his chest, but the old guy sat up again with tears streaming down his face and he snickered uncontrollably. Jack let out a quick breath. Damned fool was just laughing at his own jokes again.

The boy grinned a toothless grin at Jack. 'You can sit here next to me. I usually save this seat for Barkuss, but he doesn't really need it. He's a dog.'

Jack looked to the old man who nodded approval. Jack pushed the ever-eager dog's nose out of the way and squeezed onto his assigned seat. It was a block of dried wood of some kind, polished only by years of mealtimes. The old man set about tearing big hunks of rabbit for everyone. It seemed there was also plenty of gristle and bone to keep the dog out of their way. It scarpered off to a corner with what looked like a leg, where he splayed out on the sawdust and tore quietly at it, tail wagging into overdrive. Jack couldn't recall ever feeling as content. Which in itself was enough to snap him straight out of it. He had a long cold road ahead of him, and could afford little time with life's little luxuries.

'I have to leave today.' Jack's statement lingered in the silence. Only the sound of bones scraping tin bowls followed it. The old man's chewing slowly turned to nodding. He raised his head and looked at Jack directly.

'That's right sir. That you do. From here we'll guide you through the woods. Show you a little something, then you'll be on your way. Heavier of heart, but heavier of wisdom. Heavier of stomach too, Lord willing.' He gave Jack a little wink. The boy only stared down at his food, his mouth an angry line. Jack decided it best to leave the boy be, and steered the conversation elsewhere. Something still gnawed at him.

'I still can't recall where we met. Before yesterday that is.' Jack thought how best to ask the next question. Decided on the direct method. 'It hasn't happened for me yet has it?'

The old man stopped chewing. The boy looked up at Jack, puzzled. The old man glanced at the boy. Looked back at Jack. The early morning sun dipped behind a cloud and in that split second the old man looked as old as time.

'Boy, why don't you take the dog outside and tie him up. I reckon he needs to watch over this old place when we get going.'

'But he always comes with us. Always.'

'Not today son. Today's the day we talked about.'

The boy's eyes went wide. 'Holy shit on horse-back!' Then clamped both hands over his mouth. The old man smiled gently.

'Get to it son. Me and Jack here's got some talking to do, and we could do without little ears listening. We'll fill you in soon enough.'

Jack admired the man's parenting. He was firm but honest. And it had paid off in spades. Jack could see the boy had nothing but respect for the old man. The boy hopped off his seat and tore out of the shack, the dog bouncing at his heels. Then there was nothing but the crackle of embers beneath the cooking pot. The old man tore the meat off his second helping and chewed. A line of fat escaped his mouth and he wiped the back of his hand across his chin. He smiled at Jack.

'How long you been chasing him?'

Jack raised an eyebrow. He absent-mindedly scratched his beard. He couldn't recall when he'd last used a razor. He waited for the old man to finish chewing.

'This Devil of yours. How long? Has it been a year yet?'

Jack studied the old man. There were some things you just didn't speak of. No matter how friendly the conversation.

'As I said, I have to leave. For your safety as much as mine.' Jack stood up and stiffened his hat before putting it on. The old man nodded quietly. Seemed to ponder something in his head. Weighed up his options. When at last he spoke, the friendly drawl had vanished. His trembling hands clenched instead into steady fists on the table. His eyes seemed almost young again.

'That boy and I are one.' He paused, sat back in his chair. 'I've met you before because that boy has. That boy will grow up sooner than any boy should have to. He'll see things, do things no man alive should ever have to do. He'll do them all in your name Jack. For you. And he'd do them all again without a single regret.' A tear trickled down the old man's cheek.

Jack sat down again slowly as he realised what the old man was saying. The old man coughed, perhaps to rid a tremble in his voice. 'When I was a young boy, many years ago, a stranger came calling on our farm. He was butt naked and almost dying of thirst. My old man came out and showed the stranger some hospitality. Seemed he knew him from someplace. In the short time before things got crazy, I came to learn that the stranger was a good man. Better than good. He was pure of heart. I hadn't seen that stranger for many many years Jack. Until yesterday.'

'Does the boy know?' Jack was surprised to hear his own voice.

'That he'll grow up to be his own foster father?' The old man chuckled. 'What do you think?' He scratched the table top with a thumbnail, far away in his own thoughts.

'When will it happen for him? How?' Jack tried to run through scenarios that would allow such a catastrophe.

'That's for you to find out old friend. You have to live your life as I do mine and the boy does his. No one gets to see the future. You know that.'

Jack thought about the implications. How far back did the loop go? Would he be the cause of it?

'But I could stop it. The boy could live his life. You wouldn't need to do this. He wouldn't need to do this. Jesus, this thing could go on ...'

'Forever?' The old man smiled. 'Maybe it already has Jack. I always wanted to live forever. Just maybe not like this.' His face grew dark and he massaged his shoulder. 'Damned cold's setting in. We'd best make a move if we're to get you going.' He made a show of getting up and clamped a solid hand on Jack's shoulder. 'It's worth it you know. What you're doing. Never forget that.' he looked Jack directly in the eyes. 'You're not doing it for yourself anymore.' He gave Jack's shoulder a squeeze, offered a crooked smile and brushed past. Jack was surprised to hear him whistle on his way out. The creaking door clapped against the frame as he left.

ELEVEN

The Ox held his hat against the raging winds and knelt at the opening of a cave. Rudimentary efforts had gone into sweeping away a handful of footprints. Inside the cave, dust had recently been disturbed by a human sized inhabitant. The Ox placed his hand on a darker patch of sand and smelled his fingers. Ammonia. Strong urine. Probably severe dehydration. Maybe a day old. Two at most. The Ox got up, wiped his hands and looked around. He saw miles of nothing along the coast. Above him, gulls clamoured and bickered on a grassy cliff top. The Ox placed a foot on the rough outcrop and reached upward for a handhold.

He sensed more than heard the presence somewhere behind him. Without thinking he kicked out with all his strength against the rock and thrust himself toward the weeds on the right, spinning as he crashed into the dune. The arrow's feather clipped his ear, drawing blood in a clean line, before embedding itself into the cliff wall. The Ox used his fists to spring back up and ran toward the point of origin. As he came up out of the weeds he saw four figures coming right at him, natives, all armed to the teeth. The sun reflected off a bow as it was drawn back. The Ox put all he had into the run. Put his head down and powered his legs. He aimed for the big guy up front. Assumed he was the leader. Tried his best to ignore the arrow primed and ready to fire from the guy on the far left. He'd missed once, he could miss again. After that the guy would never miss anything again. The Ox would make sure of it.

He was less than ten yards away when the centre guy screeched. The Ox stopped his legs from moving. Made himself a dead weight and crashed to the floor. The arrow whistled above his head from the side as he smashed into the sand. He used the momentum to roll into a better position then used the inertia to kick himself back up into the run.

They were almost on top of him now, but they were slowing. The dead-fall had surprised them. It had looked like he'd died on his feet. For a second they probably thought the arrow had found its target and they had relaxed, if only for a second or two. It was human nature. Sub-conscious reactions programmed in over thousands of years. No way to bypass it. A second or two was all the Ox needed. He leaped high into the air just before impact. A man of his size and weight had no business leaping

41

anywhere but the nano-cells coursing through his bloodstream gave the Ox access to inner reserves usually only available during extreme adrenalin release.

The big leader had an axe raised above his head and a look of terror in his eyes. The Ox's leap took him directly into the projected arc of the axe's swing. The Ox removed the threat by pile-driving his fist directly into the man's collarbone as he came down. There was a loud crack, and the Ox followed with an elbow to the guy's face, breaking his nose and knocking him out cold.

One of the others screeched in from the right, thrusting forward with a long javelin. The Ox grabbed the tip, felt a white hot pain as the serrated edge cut deep into the fleshy pad at the base of his thumb. He fought an urge to release and clamped down harder on the blade. Put his other hand further along the pole and used it as a pivot point. Jerked that arm high and thrust down on the sharp tip. The native was already stretching forward as far as he could. He had no lateral strength. He was already giving everything he had into the forward thrust, nothing into the downward force. The handle end slipped up out of the native's hands and cracked the guy on the chin. The Ox spun the spear around and put the end through the guy's larynx. The Ox ignored the guy reloading the bow. Looked at the one hollering and waving the blades at him. He tore the spear back out of its owner's throat and wielded it like a baseball bat. Swung it wide and low, sliced the third guy's shins wide open. His jagged blades dropped to the ground and the guy howled like a cut pig. The Ox put him out of his misery with a boot to the groin and a sharp knee to the chin. At least he could sleep as he bled out.

The man with the bow had at last managed to find and load a third arrow and with trembling hands aimed it at the Ox. Damn it. Too far away for any kind of close combat.

The Ox re-evaluated his position, and threw the spear down. Spread his arms wide and looked the American directly in the eyes. Spoke to him firmly but quietly.

'Niye takpah tokahe. Mak U takuon takuwe.' *You attacked first. Give me a reason why.*

The Native American's expression wavered, but he doubled the tension in the bow and aimed it directly at the Ox's large chest.

'Wakin sni takuon wanasa pi wa maka ska.' *Need no reason to hunt animal.*

The Ox's hand throbbed. Droplets of blood spattered onto the sand below. He licked a single bead of dark black blood from his finger tip.

'Sni wa maka ska. Wakatanka.' *I'm not an animal. I am a god.*

The coppery taste of his own blood exploded in his mouth, and the Ox dissolved out of existence. His clothes fell to the floor in a heap. The Native American cried out in surprise and stepped back. He stepped forward and prodded the clothes with his bow. A few moments passed. The Indian whirled around in all directions. The Ox man was nowhere. He stepped back another step. Behind him the air shifted and grew warm. The Ox's naked ghost shimmered into a solid entity. His eyes empty, his face a mask of pain. He seemed a little older. His features drawn and haggard, his hair touched with flecks of white. He fell to the floor with an in-human scream. The American whirled around in terror. Emptied his bladder and ran faster than he had ever run before. The Ox arched his back in spasm and howled at the sun with pain and fury. His screams echoed against the cliffs, and only the crashing of waves answered his mournful cries.

On the far side of the beach, high on a cliff top, a young American Indian girl on horseback looked down upon the beach. She had watched as the white man vanished like a spirit and re-formed into a howling banshee. The men he had slain had not been of her tribe but they were her neighbours. They were strong men. Warriors. The white ghost had made fools of them and defeated the last one with magic. She would report back to the Grey Wolf. She had finally found what he had spoken of since she was a child. She had found the Buffalo God. Grey Wolf would be pleased with her news. She clicked her tongue and dragged the horse around. She willed the horse to go as fast as it could. They had a lot of ground to cover before nightfall.

TWELVE

Jack stood in the doorway and pumped his fist in a clenching motion. A trickle of dark red blood dripped from the tiny incision he'd made on his forearm into a small canteen. He saw the old man and the boy fussing over the dog in the distance. They'd tied it to the usual post, an ever-faithful guardian of their property. It made Jack uneasy that they were spending so long with it.

Jack shook the canteen, heard the sloshing of liquid at the bottom. Enough for an emergency at least. He resisted the temptation to suck his wound clean and plugged the canteen shut. He strapped it to his belt along with the makeshift knife he'd been given by the old man. He pitched his hat forward and rolled down his sleeve. The blood was already congealing and the cut would be camouflaged by the dark sleeve even if it bled a while longer. He took one final look at the wooden dwelling and made his way toward his new travelling companions.

'All set?' The old man's eyes were clenched shut against the bright sunlight. He ruffled the dog's head one last time and whispered something in its ear. The dog licked its master's face and the old man wiped away a tear. He cleared his throat and walked away briskly. The boy shrugged at Jack and hugged the dog goodbye.

'See you later Barkuss.' The dog had already lost interest and was chasing a fat bee around the pole. The boy chuckled and grabbed Jack's hand. They walked on after the old man, who was already at the far end of the field, striding ahead with purpose.

'How far are we going mister?' The boy's nose was crinkled and his eyes blinked against the sun as he craned his neck up toward Jack.

'As far as it takes son.'

The boy thought about this for a moment. 'You're not from around here are you?'

Jack looked down at the boy as they walked. 'Anyone ever tell you you're a real smart kid?' The boy just shrugged his shoulders.

'How fast can you run?' Jack pointed at the old man in the distance. 'Want to see if you can outrun an old horse like me?'

The boy grinned, and took off, laughing all the way. Jack smiled and looked back at the farm. The dog was nothing but a dot in the distance. Far behind it, over the mountains, dark clouds rolled in. Jack pulled his coat tighter and turned his collar up. Up ahead, the boy had caught up to the old man and was clinging to him. They walked on together, away from the coming storm. And Jack followed.

THIRTEEN

President Ben Freeman strapped himself into one of two open and illuminated pods. He closed the larger glass hatch, leaving only the service tray open so he could speak to the General.

'Christ Jim, let's go. 60 seconds and counting. Get the hell in there.'

The General flicked a final switch and closed the control panel he was working on. Instead of moving forward he stepped back and away from the time pods. 'I'm sorry Ben. I had no choice.'

The President took a second to realise what was going on. He touched his palm to the door release mechanism. The door remained closed. An electronic voice spoke over the speaker system. 'Unauthorized personnel. Please begin double clearance procedure to exit pod.' The President looked directly below him for the manual pod release. He tore the safety straps off and yanked on the yellow and black lever. Again, nothing. No way out.

'Unauthorized personnel. Please begin double clearance procedure to activate pod.'

The President's mind raced through what he knew of the security system's details. He kept an eye on the General as he did so. His old friend was backtracking slowly away toward the barricaded exit.

'They promised not to hurt you Ben. They just need you out of the way until they find Jack. He's putting us all at risk. He's changing things.'

'Dammit Jim, did that synthetic look like she was coming here to cuff me? Think, soldier! We're both dead men here. Get in that fucking pod and get us both the hell out of here.'

'I'm sorry Ben. It's too late. They're here.'

Ben heard boots on the other side of the door. Ten men, maybe more.

Ben let his mind drift away to a calmer place. Let the solution come to him instead of chasing after it. He was in a quiet white space. He saw the stars winking at him far above. The soothing voice repeated that he was an unauthorized personnel. The voice knew he was there because he was on camera. He was being analysed by A.I. Security cameras. He was unauthorized because he was the highest class threat level. He was the President of the New United States. Too high a risk of kidnap. He needed double clearance just to take a leak in this place. The pistol in his belt made it difficult to lean back comfortably and the President's focus switched to the new irritation. He snapped instantly back to attention, grabbed the gun and aimed it through the service tray at the General.

The General stopped moving. His hand hovered inches from unlocking the blocked exit.

'You won't kill me Ben.'

'I don't have to kill you Jim. Just shoot you.' The President fired. The bark of the old revolver was deafening in the enclosed space. The General sat down hard on the floor. He looked disbelievingly at the red flower blooming on his white shirt. Gut shot. Ben grimaced at the sight. It would hurt like hell until the medics got a hold of him, but he'd live to bitch about it. Besides, it would protect him from implications of collusion.

The electronic voice boomed again. 'Suspension of Presidential status, effective immediately, pending internal inquiry into attempted murder charge of General Jim Daniels. Virtual Witness iD: AI_324x300. The Vice President to assume President's role pending manual verification.'

So far so good. Ben hoped the security loophole still existed. He shut the service tray hatch and strapped himself in. Checked his blood levels, flicked two oxygen switches to manual and adjusted the pressure of the pod. Ben squatted down and held onto the release handle. Outside, the sound of a laser cutter fired up and a thin smoking line cut horizontally across the top of the laboratory entrance. It was now or never. Closing his eyes, Ben heaved on the lever. A hissing sound filled the Pod and the undercarriage rumbled beneath him. The voice spoke clearly over the machinery.

'Elite Number 1003, Ben Freeman, cleared for launch. Initiating thrusters.' Ben blew out a sigh of relief and tightened his straps. Now that he was no longer President his clearance level had automatically revoked back down to its previous lower level. President Ben Freeman may be under investigation, but Elite Soldier Ben Freeman wasn't. And Elite Soldier Ben Freeman had a Code Green clearance. Awarded for outstanding acts of bravery in the line of duty. Outside the glass pod, the General crawled away from the double doors, seeking the shelter of an upturned desk. The pod sunk down into the floor compartment. Before being entombed in the darkness of the torpedo tube, Ben saw the weakened lab door implode and black smoke pour in. Then the pod's top section became flush with the lab floor, there was a loud clank, a sudden rush of air and a sharp drop into free-fall. Then nothing but silence.

The pod's boosters kicked in and spun the pod around to its horizontal flight position. Through the front panel of glass, Ben watched as the monstrosity of the space station shrank away. Everywhere else he looked, he saw only stars.

FOURTEEN

The man closest to the Ox woke up with a broken shoulder and a broken face. He shook the red stars from his vision and grabbed a blade with his good arm. He took in the scene quickly. He saw that the large white man had been robbed of his clothes and was rolling in pain. Good. He would die a swift death. The white buffalo had beaten two of his men, and frightened away another, but not him. Never him. Big Hawk was the strongest of all men. He had killed stronger buffalo than this by himself.

The Ox clawed at his own face, his mind tearing itself apart as the neurons struggled to re-balance. Big Hawk positioned himself behind the Ox and grabbed him by the hair. The Ox screamed in rage, but Big Hawk held on, using only the forearm muscles of his damaged arm. He brought the knife down under the white buffalo's throat and screeched at the heavens. The Ox's eyes rolled in his head. He fought to clear his mind. He felt the blade's edge cut into his neck. He focused everything he had into one planned motion. A single, solid jerk upwards. He put his whole body and mind into the move, ready to smash his head into the Indian's face. He'd likely get cut in the process but it was the best chance he had. He tensed a fraction of a second before the manoeuvre, and Big Hawk sensed it. He pushed the Ox's face deep into the wet sand. The Ox's mind shattered into a thousand pieces and he could only watch numbly as the waves crashed onto the shore in the distance. His internal pain filled his mind with darkness.

The Ox used his last reserves to twist around clumsily. He would at least look his killer in the eye. Blood from his neck wound smeared across his face as he did so.

Big Hawk raised his knife high in the air. The Ox licked his lips in fear and watched the Indian plunge the blade down for the kill. Then there was nothing.

FIFTEEN

Ben wrestled with the pod's controls as it bucked and weaved through the asteroid field. He was already soaked through with sweat and his heart thumped inside his chest like a jackrabbit. He knew it was nothing to do with the capsule's thermostat or the exertion of manual control. Ben Freeman was terrified of flying. Always had been, always would be.

The Space Station was nothing more than a silent line of bright lights in the distance. His oxygen levels dipped dramatically as the craft was struck by one then another large fragment of rock. He saw a thin trail of white gas drift past his window. *Great.* It was the second time it had happened in as many minutes. He flicked the shut-offs for the remaining supply and diverted the air along the last remaining emergency channel. The gauges levelled out. His mind tried to race back through what had just unfolded on the ship and their implications but his combat training helped him block it out. *Reminiscing could come later, soldier.* Right now there was more than enough to do to get out of this in one piece. He tried to relax for the long journey toward Earth. He let his mind wander across the control panels.

His blood levels showed a lower concentration than he hoped of the catalyst nano-cells. A high percentage were dormant by way of design of course. These were for the return journey. Activated only when orally re-ingested, they would bring him closer to home and were the exact opposite of the ones that were initialized in his blood stream right now. The dormant ones, when activated through consumption, would act as blockers to the initial launch catalyst. Each dosage would bring him a step closer back to his own time. A large enough dose of blockers would bring him right back to the present. It was all theoretical of course. Earth was currently in no shape for a time traveller to leap back to. Only a small percentage of the Earth was now hospitable at all, thanks to huge thermo-sealed colonies. And the leaper's safety nets, the oceans, were all unpredictable no-go zones since the war. Their new temperature ranges fluctuated constantly. A man could boil or freeze to death as soon as he arrived. There was also the additional complication of consuming such a large dosage of blockers. The recovery period from such a dose would render the traveller incapacitated for a lengthy window of time, leaving him particularly vulnerable to external threats. This brought Ben's thoughts crashing back to his old friend the

General. His mind wandered to their first meeting. How could a man with such vision suddenly become so blind?

Outside the pod, the thrusters flickered intermittently, constantly correcting the flight path at the macroscopic level. Another fist sized rock bounced lazily into their path, scraping against the underbelly. It took out two primary sensors before slicing open a protected section of hose further along the hull.

For the third and final time during the flight, an air line ruptured, and the white exhaust quietly hissed out in a thin trail, undetected by the disabled CPU.

SIXTEEN

General Daniels had always been a great thinker. The young Jim Daniels that Ben had first met had been a brilliant young mind who had joined the battlefield simply to satisfy a brain that longed to excel. No longer satisfied with books and theory he had an all-consuming urge to take part in the real world. He had known he was the best he could be mentally, and wanted to match that achievement physically. His peers and superiors had tried to bring him down, to break him at every turn, and they had failed. Ben had seen this at first hand and had witnessed the man's mental strength. His sheer will power triumphed over his physical limitations.

It had been Daniels' brain child to build the pods that would deliver a time traveller safely to a position just above the poisonous Earth before he leaped. It was such a simple yet elegant solution. Typical of the General's lateral thinking.

The General, a newly qualified Elite back then, and barely a day after graduating, had seen three men from his old platoon killed in as many hours. Time-leaping was in its infancy and huge rudimentary installations allowed the test soldiers to leap back a week or so at a time. Missions were hashed together on the battlefield perimeters under heavy fire.

The three doomed volunteers had leaped back one after the other. The original mission had been trivial on paper. Leap back, recon the enemy position three days prior and go dark. Then simply wait out the ensuing battle before reporting back at the initial launch point. To the scientists at the launch site, the soldiers would disappear momentarily before returning on foot moments later with the information required. For the soldier it meant a headache and covert foot patrols for a week, before catching up naturally with their regular timeline, barely a week older for their efforts.

When the first volunteer failed to report back he was listed as MIA. Another was quickly sent with the additional secondary mission to recover information about the first. When a third had to be sent with a similar briefing, Daniels was the first to work out what had happened.

He had approached his superiors and explained his theory. They brought in a makeshift scanner-digger and eventually found the soldiers' pulped bodies intertwined barely 3 feet below ground some hundred yards away from the launch site. Their limbs crushed into a black soup by the immense pressure of rock and clay. Recognisable only by their DNA samples, the men had all been awarded posthumously for their bravery and the details of their demise quickly erased from all records.

Under the stresses of war the scientists had overlooked the fact that the landscape had shifted during the last onslaught. Terrain had been levelled by both sides, craters had formed, plates had shifted. The elevation of the launch site itself was down an average of ten feet per week. Following such an oversight, combined with the fact that they didn't have a clue as to why the soldiers had landed some distance away, the scientists had little choice but to agree to listen to the young Daniels' detailed proposals.

Daniels was awarded full temporary co-operation by the military. Word had gotten out and orders from above ensured his access to help improve the Leap Project. He was transferred to the Darka Medi-Labs, albeit under the watchful eyes of his superiors.

Early prototypes had been modified hover drones. Floating well above the margins of error the time-pods had been flown above the terrain, the subjects equipped with parachutes for a safe arrival. Of course it quickly became apparent that nothing could leap back with the soldier, including parachutes or safety nets. A couple of broken legs and some lateral thinking later, Daniels initiated testing above the swamplands. Success rates were higher but still not perfect. The injury rates were found to be directionally proportional to the timespan leaped. If the timeframe became too great, the soldiers were sometimes found to land several metres away from the water's edge along the Earth's axis, their legs shattered on the hard ground. This broke Daniels's heart and he re-doubled his efforts. Men were being hurt because of his shortcomings. He went into a dark mood of isolation. He cancelled all further testing for a period of 48 hours as he pored over the research data. His furious superior officers became agitated and frustrated. They demanded he continued testing, regardless of collateral damage. Their war couldn't wait a single second, let alone two days. They threatened him with dishonourable expulsion, arrest, and much worse. He stared them all out, stood his ground and eventually went above their heads. After being passed from one department to the next he finally got through to the head office. He explained to the company chairman's aide directly that he only needed two days and he would have their Leap Project ready for action. Promised them safe leaps of several years instead of weeks. All they had to do was give him two days, uninterrupted by political and physical threats or bureaucratic red tape. The company man thanked him for the refreshingly frank and brutally honest telephone call and said someone would be in touch.

The next day at 6 am a young recruit rapped on his door with an envelope for him. Inside was a new security clearance badge and a note. The badge promised him unlimited company resources under his direct command for seven full days. The note promised him a court marshall and a long military trial for insubordination and treason if he failed to deliver. He was under no illusions as to the severity of this threat. He was in well over his head and it was now all or nothing. His superior officers had been quietly transferred during the night and he was given a fresh team of dedicated scientists from across the globe.

Their first priority was to iron out the flaws in the spatial delivery. Daniels worked through the first night going through every scrap of information he could find on the subject. He went back to his early days and reverted to rubber-duck debugging of the puzzle. He forced himself to explain the situation out loud, step by step, as if explaining it to an inanimate object with no previous knowledge of the problem. The theory was that in comparing the expected result at each point with the actual result it would quickly become apparent at which stage the logic failed.

The soldiers were somehow being relocated not only in time but also in space. Daniels broke the problem down into parts and went back to the beginning. It had long been established that space and time were directly linked. Since its inception, time travel theory had gone under the assumption that a man's path in time would be rigidly attached to his path through space. Say a man planned to stand on a rock in the desert for two days. If you approached that man at the start of day one and sent him through time to near the end of day two, he would disappear from your perceived reality and appear again almost two days later on that very same rock. Daniels knew that what was actually happening indicated that the man would not appear on the rock but at a different location, seemingly linked to the rotation of the earth. The man would also most likely be buried under sand. Two problems, two deviations. X and Y axes.

The problem along the vertical Y axis was easily explained by changes in terrain height between now and the point of arrival. Launching above water was a quick and dirty but inexpensive fix for this. Even with miscalculations for terrain height, a leaper who arrived too low would only get wet and not become entombed in solid rock. And the company loved inexpensive fixes, no matter how quick or dirty. Daniels already planned to recommend that leaps only occur above ocean territories from then on.

The real problem he had was with the positional deviation across the land - the X axis. If there were to be any real improvements in Leap duration as he had promised, he had to be able to predict exactly how far along the Earth's surface the Soldiers would travel before landing. Otherwise even launching above the middle of the Ocean could not guarantee a wet landing. The question was why it was happening at all.

A young Ben Freeman had been unable to sleep that night. Newly graduated as an Elite operative, he'd been awarded 72 hours downtime to debrief and prepare for his first mission. He'd been outside his trailer, smoking his second cigar of the evening. Just looking at the stars and taking stock of his life. Over the horizon he could see the green glow of battle raging on as it did every night. He was always amazed at how beautiful it looked from a distance. A chain link fence bordered his trailer's perimeter and the Darka-Labs. Sometimes the white coats came out for a smoke and they exchanged pleasantries through the wire. Ben hadn't seen anyone for a few days. Rumour had it that something big had gone down. A few of the boys had volunteered for some top secret recon shit and had shipped out to the battlefield with a truckload of white coats. The brainy kid Daniels had also gone into the facility after them. There had been some shouting and cursing, and the kid hadn't come back.

Ben was halfway through the vintage cuban when a fire door opened on the other side of the chain-link and Daniels came out. He wore standard issue dark Elite combat trousers, and a two-tone black vest that was soaked through with perspiration. He wore a white lab coat tied clumsily around his waist. He ran his hands through his hair and sat heavily on the asphalt with his back to the red bricks. It took him a moment to notice Ben, and he nodded politely. Ben held up the cuban in return. Daniels wiped a hand over his face then pushed himself up off the floor.

'Busy night?' Ben handed him the cigar through the fence.

'Terrible.' Daniels's eyes were red rimmed. He closed his eyes and pulled hard on the tobacco. His usual boyish charms were nowhere to be seen.

Ben nodded at Daniels's Elite uniform. 'You too then?'

Daniels exhaled a mouthful of clean white smoke. 'An army of two.' He grinned.

'Three.' Ben watched the green flashes in the distance. 'Silent Jack deployed early yesterday. Cancelled his allocated leave time and requested immediate transfer into the Green Zone. Seems he couldn't wait to get stuck in.'

Daniels raised an eyebrow and tapped his own temple. 'Hate to see how that clock works.'

Ben looked over at the dark Med-Lab buildings. A clinical white light streamed out through the open fire door. 'So what *can't* you tell me about your project in there?'

'Everything. They'd shoot you for even knowing there *was* a project.' Daniels looked deadly serious. Ben let out a low whistle.

'Heavy shit huh?' He winked at Daniels. 'Anything I can help you with Hawkings?'

'Not unless you can disprove Einstein's most thoroughly proven theorem, and apply that to a machine we haven't even built yet.' He glanced nervously at the patrolman guarding the Med-Lab entrance gate in the distance. He rubbed his eyes with his knuckles. Right then Ben thought how lucky he was to be just another set of feet on the ground. He hated all the politics that came with warfare.

Daniels looked up at the stars, took one last drag of the cigar and dropped it by his feet.

'I guess I'll see you out in the field, Freeman.' His smile was weighed down by a world of responsibility.

Ben gave a friendly salute. 'Hope you work out whatever it is you're trying to fix.'

'Oh that? I already have.' Jim Daniels smiled, crushing the embers underfoot. 'I just came out to celebrate.' His smile changed into an infectious grin and both men laughed. They laughed without really knowing why. Perhaps just because they could. In those days they were invincible, as only the youthful truly can be.

Ben watched Daniels head back to his work and shook his head in admiration. He took one last look at the stars and, still smiling, thought he would sleep just fine after all.

SEVENTEEN

The mid-morning sun had long disappeared. Jack hadn't been surprised when the drops of rain had turned to sleet, and as they reached the high ground, to fat flakes of snow. The sky was a constant dull grey and visibility was minimal. The old man still bulldozed on ahead, using a stick when the incline got too rough. The boy had kept up most of the way but now sat astride Jack's shoulders, issuing warnings whenever a low branch approached.

The long walk had been uneventful for the most part. They'd had a few false alarms, mainly thanks to the old man's jitters. They'd crouched low and silent for the best part of ten minutes at one point because a deer was following them.

The boy grew suddenly heavy on Jack's back and his breathing became a steady rhythm. Jack strode forward and walked level with the old man.

'I never asked your name.'

The old man grinned, spat out a snowflake. 'I've always been called Sonny. Before the old man arrived back then, I was probably something else. I don't rightly recall.' He smiled. 'After that, just Sonny or Son. I guess it's the only thing I can call the boy without feeling a little strange about it.'

'It's why you call me Sir instead of Jack. You still see me as an elder don't you.' Jack couldn't help but be intrigued by the situation. The old man winced and stopped to take a breath. He looked at the sleeping boy, his younger self, and smiled.

'None of us ever really grow up into the adults we seem on the outside do we Jack. We all carry our childhood demons forever.'

Jack pulled his collar higher. Up ahead the ground evened out and promised the shelter of trees. The old man looked to where Jack was looking. A layer of frosting mottled the grass ahead, and a little snow had begun to take hold.

'I guess we're almost there after all.' Old Sonny managed a crooked smile. 'It's been such a long journey – I guess I've never really thought about reaching the end.'

Jack suddenly felt as if he were back on the battlefield, and forced his heart to slow a little. He quickly scanned the perimeter, but saw nothing. Nothing but the steady fall of snowflakes. Old Sonny sensed his unease and put a comforting arm on his shoulder.

'Not quite yet dear Jack. Not quite yet. Come. We're almost at the wall.' He continued through the opening in the trees and into the woods, a new spring in his step.

And Jack carried the boy in after him.

EIGHTEEN

Young Sergeant Rogers was tired. He looked at the orange light of the clock on the dash. 1:20 am. He had twenty five minutes left and only the pleasure of a hormonal wife to greet him when he got home. Oh, the joy of it. The rhythm of the windshield wipers had already sent his partner Hodgson to sleep. Rogers marvelled how a man could sleep so much. Maybe he was diabetic. He made a mental note to rib him about cutting down on the candy.

It had been a quiet night overall. A couple of DUI's and a domestic. Nothing major. Maybe they had the rain to thank for that. It hadn't stopped for six hours straight. Rogers squelched the radio as they cruised past the construction site.

'Dispatch, this is 48. I need a 10-9 on that address.'

The radio buzzed. A mischievous female voice replied. '48, a 184 Heaton. Old age setting in 48?' Rogers smiled. Clara. The fact she was deviating from protocol was a good sign. He hadn't overstepped the mark with her last night after all. Or maybe he was just grasping at straws now that things had gone to shit at home.

'48, 10-97.' He clipped the radio back on the dash.

Rogers had married his high school sweetheart at 20, and now at the grand old age of thirty one, the pressures of their jobs and his reluctance to want a family seemed to bring out the worse in the both of them. Every conversation had become a battle, and they had become strangers living in the same house. He was tired of it. Tired of his life. He eased the Crown Vic to a halt and nudged Hodgson in the ribs. He popped the lights.

'Cinderella. Let's go.'

'Sleeping beauty, numb-nuts.' Hodgson stretched and grinned. 'Christ, how long was I out? Feels like a camel took a dump in my mouth.' The car shook as he maneuvered to wipe the doughnut sugar from his uniform creases.

'Lost a little weight there Hodge?'

'Screwing your wife keeps me below my target man, you know that.'

Rogers smiled in the dark. He took the Maglite from the dash and walked out into the strobing blue and red thrown by the roof lamps. The call had come in three minutes previously. A homeless man in some kind of trouble. No third parties involved. Witnesses had seen him from the overpass. Rogers blinked against the heavy rain. Should have worn his poncho. Where were the damn medics? He hated this part of the job. First on scene always got the worst of it. He heard a siren in the distance and relaxed a little. Hodgson went to the trunk and put on his waterproofs. He looked like an oversized fisherman. Rogers unclipped his gun and shimmied through a workman's ad-hoc opening in the high mesh fence.

'Are you kidding me?' Hodgson looked in dismay at the size of the site entrance. 'I'll meet you in there. Must be a more formal way in.' He blinked against the downpour. 'I'll check the perimeter en route.'

'Roger that. Blip me in 5.' Roger went ahead, holding his flashlight in front, his other hand shielding his eyes from the weather. He unclipped his radio and pressed the talk button. He heard a squelch and then a whine. Reminded him of amp feedback. *Dammit. Weather-proof my ass.*

The construction site was only a partial build. Rogers thought it looked like ground zero had a few years ago. It was a huge flat area surrounded by high boards and fencing. Alternating piles of rubble and deep trenches made up most of the space. Huge concrete pipe sections stuck out of the ground here and there. Either ready to be put in or old ones being dug out. Steel rods outlined proposed foundations. No machinery. No diggers or dumpsters. Rogers thought maybe the project had been postponed, or was in-between contractors. He'd heard a lot of similar stories these past couple years. The economy was going to shit, that was for sure. He was deep in this train of thought when his four-cell flashed across a mannequin. It was only the top half, and was almost completely covered in grey mud. Then the mannequin's eyes opened and looked right at Rogers. Rogers jumped and his breath hitched in his throat.

The figure's eyes lolled back in its head and it let out a blood curdling wail. Rogers leaped back with a yelp and dropped his flashlight into the mud, plunging him into a terrible darkness.

NINETEEN

'Wake the boy up. He needs to remember this.' Old Sonny had followed a snaking dry stone wall to the base of a grand old tree. He was looking up at it as if trying to establish how high it climbed. Jack grabbed the dozing child and hoisted him up over his head. The boy awoke on the way down and groaned. He yawned as he was set on the ground and looked around blearily.

'Is this the place?' The boy's hair stood up at the back and Jack was painfully reminded of what little childhood the boy would get to enjoy.

'Sure looks like it. It seems smaller than I remember but maybe that's just my eyes being bigger these days.' The old man gave a half hearted smile. He seemed a little unsteady. He knelt down, looked up at the tree, and ran a shaking hand across his own face as if remembering something.

Jack looked up at the gnarled old Oak. It sure looked the part, whatever this was about. The tree stood out a mile from all the others. The old man walked around the thick dark trunk, looking upwards the whole time he did so.

'This tree will be important. To both of you.' The old man turned and knelt down next to the boy. 'Son, when it is eventually time, this is the tree. When you see her next on your travels, she'll be but a baby tree. You won't understand that right now. But it's important that you remember her. And that you mind what I'm telling you.' The boy looked confused. He shrugged and risked a mischievous glance at Jack. The old man's eyes opened wide and he struck the boy hard across the face with an open hand. The boy yelped in fright and pain. His eyes welled up and he looked up at Old Sonny with such fear and heartbreak that even Jack found himself moved.

The old man gripped the boy by the shoulders and shook him once, hard. Old Sonny's eyes were glazed with tears and spittle flew from his mouth as he spoke. 'You'll never know how much it killed me to do that, and I know you'll never trust me fully again. But know this,' He tilted the boy's red face up to look at his own. 'This tree will remind you forever, that I was once your Pa. And your Pa loved you with all his heart.' The boy wept a child's tears, his chest hitching and his breath caught in his throat. The old man pulled him into a tight embrace and whispered in his ear. 'I love you son.'

60

He pushed the boy back to arm's length and studied him. He wiped a tear from the boy's cheek with a weathered thumb and stroked the hair out of his eyes. 'Now don't you ever forget this God forsaken tree. This wall won't always be here to guide you.'

'I won't Pa, I'm sorry.' The boy's words slurred out amongst more tears, and the old man tousled the lad's hair and spoke with a softness that Jack hadn't heard in him before. 'There's nothing to be sorry about my boy. You always did real good.'

He wiped his own face and cleared his throat. Jack noticed he kept one arm tightly around the boy's shoulder as he got up. Maybe he was scared that if he let the boy go, he'd never get to hold him again.

The old man pointed up past Jack and high into the tree. 'Your part in this lies way up there Jack. In a knot hole no bigger than your fist. How are you at climbing trees stranger?' The old man's colour had come back a little, and Jack was relieved to see that the boy too was a little curious, wrinkling his nose up at the tree's nooks and crannies.

Jack was about to hoist himself up when an idea hit him. He looked up at the thick branches and with a sharp intake of breath gave the old man his most solemn look.

'I don't think I can do it. Seems awful high to me. I'm not much of a climber.' He shrugged at them both. The boy's eyes lit up, but he held his tongue. His confidence had been shattered.

Old Sonny looked like he was about to scold the soldier's ineptitude but a look from Jack stopped him. The old man's eyes narrowed. He looked at little Sonny and saw what Jack saw in the boy's face. Old Sonny's own eyes lit up in understanding.

'Well, I certainly can't climb her. May as well ask me to climb to the moon. Oh well. I guess that's that then. We tried at least.' The old man turned away from the tree.

'I can do it.' The boy spoke a little more timidly than usual, but Jack saw his usual fire just beneath the surface.

The old man feigned surprise, as if he'd forgotten the boy was even there.

Jack mimed uncertainty. 'It's a real man's job I reckon. I wouldn't want a boy like you to hurt himself. What are you, five, six?' Jack laid it on thick and hoped he wasn't overdoing it.

'I'll be seven next month. And I can climb that tree better than you ever could mister.'

'That's right, he is Jack. And if my boy here says he can climb the damned tree, then I believe in him.' Old Sonny smiled a thank you at Jack, and the boy grinned up at his old man, his faith in him returning.

Jack shrugged and scratched his head. 'Well alright, but if he manages it, I guess we won't have no boy travelling with us after that. He'll be a man for sure.'

The boy's chest swelled fit to burst and he bolted for the tree. The old man squeezed Jack's arm in gratitude. Jack touched the brim of his hat, *don't mention it*. He wondered briefly if the old man remembered climbing the tree when he was a boy, or in his version if Jack had done it.

The boy made short work of getting into the first batch of thick branches. He paused to evaluate his position and scanned the trunk for the next foot hold.

'Where's the hole Pa?'

'See that crooked branch, the one that forks into two like a snake's tongue?'

'The high one? But no one could reach that! It's a mile up.'

'Well, I guess we could try asking a passer by ...' Old Sonny had to hide his smile with his hand as he spoke. The boy didn't reply, he just gritted his teeth and swung up onto the next level.

Before too long, the boy was so far up that only the swaying branches gave his position away. Jack saw the old guy's face strain to make out young Sonny's progress. There was a moment of silence from above before the shriek of excitement.

'I found it! I got it Pa!'

The old man clasped both hands together in a knot and his lower lip trembled in a smile. 'Careful now, you hear me Sonny? Shimmy it into your britches. Mind you use both hands to come down to me.'

The boy did just that. Jack couldn't help but be impressed as he watched him descend. The boy seemed born to climb. Looking up at the sheer scale of the tree, he wondered how quickly he could have done it himself. He figured he'd still be on his way up, and complaining all the way at that.

Jack and the old man gave the boy a helping hand from the lowest drop and he landed on his knees in the dirt. He smiled up at them, and they grinned right back. Jack was especially pleased that the boy, now a man in his own eyes, clutched at his old man's coat tails once more. A young man maybe, but still someone's son.

The boy took out a thin rectangular package from behind his back. Jack saw that it had been wrapped in a rag of some sort. The old man took it gently from the boy and bent down and hugged him tight.

'Well done my boy.'

The boy beamed, but his curiosity was getting the better of him. 'What's in it?'

The old man laughed and held the package up to Jack. 'Well that's for Jack to say. It's his package after all.' Jack pushed up the brim of his hat and took the parcel. It didn't look familiar. Jack saw that it was wrapped in oiled sheepskin, not a rag after all. It weighed very little and had some give in it but not much. Sturdy, but not solid. Jack unwrapped the sheepskin.

Droplets of rain danced across it as he did so, the watertight cover reluctant to absorb the moisture. Both Sonny's, old and young, watched eagerly as Jack took out the object.

It was a small black book. The leather covers bound together by a weathered dark leather strap. Jack ran his fingers across an etching on the back. He recognised it as a brand name. A registered trademark from a time just before his. Inside the back cover was a paper pouch, to store loose folds of paper and such.

The book had maybe a hundred yellowing pages, still dry and unspoiled. Jack leafed through to the front. He frowned. The old man's mouth hung open. The boy's smile faded. Jack thumbed through again the the other way. Saw the same result.

The black book's pages all had the same thing in common.

They were all completely blank.

TWENTY

'Connor, leave that.' Carla Walker was tired, hungry and hungover.

They were making slow progress through the flea market that sprawled through the south side every Saturday morning. What had begun as a short-cut home from the grocery store had turned into a battle through the crowds of the market. Connor was eleven years old and interested in everything. He was four steps behind her and elbow deep in a box of dusty books. He had seen an old comic annual on the top and was lost in the promise of childhood heroes. He looked at the price scrawled in crayon on a carton flap.

'It's only 50 cents ma. Please?' He held the thick book close to his chest, willing her to see how much he wanted it.

'Connor. Drop it.' A pause. 'Let's go.' She peered over her dark glasses, and raised an eyebrow. He knew that look. He sighed and placed the book back onto the pile.

'Grab one of these bags would you, they're killing your old ma.' She handed him the heaviest of the three brown paper sacks and re-adjusted her fingers through the remaining handles.

Connor blew a lock of hair from his eyes and forgot about the book. He knew she didn't mean to be the way she was. Things had been difficult for her since dad left.

'Ma?' he stole a glance up at her as he hurried to keep up. She didn't answer, she was on the tips of her toes, trying to find the side street entrance up ahead. People were a solid mass. A gap opened up, making a lane through the crowd. Connor heard a siren somewhere in the background.

'Keep up now champ, I think I see the alley we want.' She pushed ahead through a family of tourists, aiming for the gap. Connor's bag snagged on a pushchair and he dropped his gaze for a moment. When he turned back his mother had disappeared. The tourist unfolded his map, giving Connor zero visibility. Connor pushed past the map, his heart quickening. The siren was much louder now. Up ahead he could hear shouting and commotion. He heard the thud of some heavy objects. Sounded like the garbage men that woke him every week. Maybe they collected late morning in this part of town. He still couldn't see through the swarm of limbs. He squeezed through, pulling his bag awkwardly after him. An apple tumbled from the top of it, and bounced away from him, rolling into the clearing ahead. Connor saw it roll over road markings.

He saw that the market actually occupied two sides of a single-lane of blacktop. He assumed cars used it every now and then when the people got out of the way. Maybe it was for deliveries and cabs. The apple rolled to the centre, it stopped short of someone who had fallen over. The apple bumped against a dark shoe, lying forgotten some distance away from the pedestrian. An ambulance was already on site. Connor thought it was parked somewhat clumsily on the far kerb, and he noticed its front tyre was flat. A wisp of white smoke seeped from the grill. Connor realised that other groceries also littered the road. The garbage collectors must have been in a rush.

He looked to the other side, desperately looking for his mother. His hands were clammy now. Something about the scene upset him. His heart beat a little too quickly. A paramedic stumbled out of his driver's seat. Connor looked in horror as the man vomited all over his uniform. He had a gash on his head and swayed like a drunk. Connor's mind pieced the scene together backwards. The shoe. The thud. The siren. A busy open road through a crowd of people.

A second paramedic groaned from the passenger side of the vehicle. They weren't here because of the accident, they were the cause of the accident. Tins of hot dogs littered the ground. His favourite. Ma had bought him enough to last until doomsday, that's what she had said. Connor dropped the bag and ran forward.

His mother lay at an awkward angle. Her dark glasses no longer hid her eyes. There was no blood. Just a single pale blotch on her temple. Connor saw through thick tears that she still clutched the string handles, but the bags were long gone. He was vaguely aware of people rushing to help her but he also knew they were too late. He hugged his mother for the very last time. He buried his face in her hair and wept in agony.

TWENTY-ONE

The fire crackled and popped, and the three of them huddled closer to it. A bitter wind had come in from the east and they ate quickly. No meat this time, only roots and nuts. No one had spoken much since they had found the book. Jack looked deep into the fire, searching the flames for his own answers. The old man kept little Sonny warm inside his coat, and alternated between rubbing his own arms and the boy's. The boy fell asleep that way.

Jack glanced up at them both. 'Maybe this was a bad idea. I should have taken you home.'

The old man smiled. 'Then you would have killed us all.' He spat at the fire.

Jack saw the boy stir. This was still an adventure for him. Not yet the life and death brutality it had been for the old man.

'They waited for us that night. We weren't there of course. My old man knew as I did to wait out the night.' Old Sonny grimaced at what was coming next. He cleared his throat. 'That damned dog. Looked out for us to the very end. Those no good bastards.' Sonny let the thought hang in the air as he composed himself.

When the old man spoke again, his voice was but a whisper. 'I had to leave the poor mutt there. What comes next for us depends on it.' The old man wiped a knuckle across his own cheek. 'The dog took one of their hands. Bit three fingers and a thumb clean off. I found them in the dirt. All those years ago. Nothing else. They burned all of it.' He closed his eyes. 'Dog too.'

Jack hung his head low. Thought how that must have been for six year old Sonny. How it would be for him tomorrow. 'Do you know who they were?'

Old Sonny shook his head. 'What's to know is what they were after.' He pointed at Jack's coat. Jack put a protective hand over the bulge inside. The book was safe for now. How to keep it safe was another matter. Why it was important was another.

'You were as shocked as we were weren't you?' The old man had a curious glint in his eye. 'Back at the tree. You didn't expect it to be damned empty either did you?'

Jack smiled. 'I don't know what I expected. I try to take things as they come.'

Old Sonny shivered and threw another piece of thick bark onto the flames. He saw no stars above, only clouds. He cleared his throat. 'I don't remember it.' He prodded the fire, keeping his eye line away from Jack's.

'Remember what?'

'The book.' Sonny grimaced. 'I remember my old man walloping me a good one, then I remember the tree. I'll never forget that damned tree.' He scratched his cheek.

Jack saw that the boy's face still burned a dark red in the exact same spot.

Old Sonny continued. 'But I don't remember the book. Seeing the boy climb yesterday brought some of it back but after that it's blank. Until the dog.'

'You were young. I'm surprised you remember any of it.' Jack tipped the brim of his hat over his eyes and leaned back. The old man fussed with the fire.

'But I put it there. I should remember something. I feel like I used to remember, but it's fading. Like something's changed.'

Jack stirred. Pulled his coat closer around him. 'Seems like things are always changing. Guess we just have to change with them.'

The old man shivered and huddled down next to the boy. His mind hopped from one thing to the next, piecing together shreds of memories from nearly a century of events. When it came to him later that night he was almost asleep. It felt like a hammer blow to the chest. For a second he forgot to breathe. His mouth moved silently, as he considered the implications.

His memories hadn't faded. His mind had blocked them out. The human brain will do whatever it can to reduce mental trauma. A great loss or horrific injury will be locked away by the subconscious in its darkest corner. Sonny realized with a sudden great clarity and horror that the day that he'd found the book was the last day he'd ever seen his old man.

TWENTY-TWO

The young warrior Akuti waited patiently outside the Grey Wolf's dwelling. The snow still fell but did not yet make her feet cold. An elder passed by in the distance carrying fresh buck skin, and nodded in a silent greeting. Akuti smiled in return. She saw no one else around. Not many people lived near the ridge. Most of the villagers sheltered further down, where the trees were thicker. Akuti enjoyed the solitude up here. It made her feel closer to the skies.

She knew very little of the ancient one's wisdom, save that it was indeed great. The old man had always known so many things and shown them how to stand strong against others. She had been born into a community hidden deep in the highest forests, and they lived away from fear. Elder Chiefs came from long distances to seek Grey Wolf's tongue. Those who paid him kindly and heeded his words were blessed by the great Coyote and survived yet another cold year. But those who did not believe in his words soon joined the fallen. Flood, famine or battle, it didn't matter which, they fell just the same. Some had said that the Wolf was actually the great Coyote himself, such was his knowledge and strength. But she had seen Grey Wolf, and he looked like no Coyote she had ever seen. He was an ancient being, but still strong and sure. Some said he was older than the trees themselves, and she believed it. For it was not his age that was remarkable about Grey Wolf. It was the fact that Grey Wolf really did have twice the wisdom and courage of any man. For Grey Wolf had been blessed with two faces.

The wind threw a flurry of snow that whipped Akuti's legs, and she blinked up at the sky. She would remember this day. It would be the day that a prophecy was fulfilled. Grey Wolf's tales of ancient battles had entertained the village children for decades. The elders smiled politely at these musings, and knew them to be analogies for warfare and survival. Only the children knew of the truths he spoke. Akuti was the youngest warrior in the village, and the stories burned brightly in her mind.

He had spoken of an ancient battle between gods. His speaking face would say the words while the other looked on quietly. It always watched, fused to his speaking face, but never making a sound. The old man would point at the lines in the stars with his good arm as he spoke, drawing their outlines with a steady finger. His other arm always hidden inside the layers of thick deerskin.

His story would continue into the night. The Great Coyote and the Silent Buffalo had once been great allies. But the sleeping Coyote had been overcome by the Great Buffalo God, and had been cast down to Earth for his weakness. The enraptured audience scoured the heavens, looking for traces of this fierce war. Most would swear they saw the pair still locked in battle. The old man looked the children in the eyes one by one as he finished his tale. None of them dared look at his second face, which watched on silently.

The Great Buffalo God would also fall to Earth one day. Whoever took away his soul would release the Great Coyote, and he would rise again to the stars where he still belonged.

Akuti had embraced this tale the most for she had dreams that she too would one day fly to the skies she loved so much. In her dreams she soared over the land, higher than even the great Raven.

She saw that the snow fell heavier now, and when she looked up long enough, the heavy flakes became black silhouetted stars, falling to earth.

A coughing from inside the dwelling, and the thick skins covering the doorway parted. Old Grey Wolf appeared at the opening and with a single nod, beckoned her inside. She breathed out and with a quickening of her heart, walked in after him.

TWENTY-THREE

The apartment was black. The green light below the cooker told him it was a little after four. Sergeant Rogers felt blindly for the latch, clicked the door shut and dropped his keys into the empty fruit bowl. Emptied his pockets and dropped everything in on top of the keys. Shrugged off his heavy coat and belt and let them hang on a chair back to dry. He saw a note on the table, ignored it, and opened the refrigerator. He opened a Bud, and finished it in two long mouthfuls. He took another two out of the pack and grabbed some meat loaf with his other hand. Elbowed the door shut and left the room. The cat squirmed past him and he dropped heavily into his old armchair. He noticed he was still in the dark. He slugged back half of his next beer. The clock sounded ten times louder in the darkness. He finished the meatloaf in between gulps and just stared into the darkness. Exhausted. Cold. Numb. A little drunk now too. He wondered where Maria was. She hadn't called to ask why he was late. Hadn't fallen asleep with the light on this time either. The crack under their bedroom door was dark. Maybe she'd left a voicemail or a message. He remembered the note. He got up, a little unsteady, and made it back to the kitchen table without kicking the cat or spilling his beer. He nudged the wall lights on and scooped up the folded square of paper. It only had two words. He turned the paper over then flipped it back. Nothing but two words. He read them again to be sure. They still said the same thing. *I'm sorry*. He walked quickly across the room, through the living room and opened their bedroom door. Flicked on the lights. The switch made a foreign sound. A slight echo joined it. The room was bare. No floral bed-linen, no fancy drapes, no clothes, no high heeled shoes, and no Maria. Shit. He thumbed open his cell phone and hovered over her name. Then remembered the time. The cat looked up at him then rubbed against his leg. Damned cat. She could have at least taken the cat with her. He peeled off his uniform, and dropped it into the laundry basket. He yanked the shower lever to maximum heat and let the pressure work its way up to an acceptable level. The steam quickly filled the small wash room and the cat mewled briefly before finding something more interesting to do in the kitchen. He scooped out his old tattered dorm towel from the wicker basket, the only one Maria hadn't taken, and hung it on the shower rail. She had also left some shower gel. That was thoughtful of her.

No sense in getting her designer heels all wet for the sake of some soap, he guessed. The water massaged his scalp and he let his thoughts wander. They came to him silently, with only the hiss of the shower as their soundtrack. He saw the naked man in the mud, screaming silently. The blue lights popping as the medics arrived. The man clinging to him in desperation. His legs crushed and somehow packed into solid earth. The morphine shots and the oxygen mask to calm the guy down. The painstaking process of loosening the hard soil. His partner, Hodgson, vomiting as he saw what remained of the man's legs. The skin ripped to shreds, the soil and random construction debris somehow mangled with the flesh and bone. He'd almost passed out himself. Half a rusty license plate jutted out between the man's calf muscle and shin bone. The delirium as the howling man slipped in and out of consciousness on his way to Langone.

Rogers let the hot water wash away the day's craziness. His thoughts turned to his wife. His marriage was done. He had a brief idea that he should fight for it. He remembered the good days vividly. He would have died for her. The early days. But he was only hurting himself by clinging on to those memories. It was best to replace them with this last year's blackness. The eruptions he faced when he came home as she realised that another day had passed and she was still stuck with a man who would never be good enough. He wiped his face absently and from nowhere the tears came. Some of it was relief, some was certainly the three empty beers, but mostly it was just grief. He cried for something that was gone forever. Something that had once been good and pure. He slumped down in the shower and wept quietly for his lost love, with his face in his hands and the water streaming down the wall.

In the kitchen the cat licked its lips and sprang onto the kitchen table. It could smell Rogers' scent in the fruit bowl and purred as it investigated the contents: It sniffed at the bunch of keys, the money clip, and the small leather-bound black book.

TWENTY-FOUR

Jack awoke with a jolt. The sky was still dark, but something was different. The boy was fast asleep. Jack could hear his short, hitching breaths. Jack's eyes adjusted and the glowing embers of the fire became his light. He saw what was missing at once.

'Old man?' he whispered. He got on his feet instantly. He turned around a full 360 degrees but old Sonny was nowhere to be found. 'Boy. Wake up.' Little Sonny stirred and cracked open his eyes.

'Where is he? Where's Pa?' the boy stood up slowly, the cool night making him shiver. Jack held a finger to his mouth and listened. The wind sighed through the long grass and a loon whistled in the distance. No other sounds. Jack saw no signs of a struggle, but no sign that the old man had walked away either. The tall grass remained undisturbed in each direction. Jack played back the previous night's conversation. He didn't know where the old man had gone but he knew where the boy had to be soon. Had been many years ago.

'Son, quickly now, pick up that hat and your Pa's water pouch, we're going home.'

'We have to wait for Pa, we can't just ...' the boy's brow became an angry line.

'Hush now with that worrying. Your Pa told me you need to be home this morning. I guess he meant with or without him. He might already be scouting up ahead. Besides, would you mess with your old Pa if you were a wild coyote or an angry injun?'

The boy smirked at this last and seemed to soften a little. 'Nossir!'

A cloud drifted a little in the East, opening up a small slit of moonlit sky and the boy's face looked so lost that it hurt Jack's heart. Jack placed his own coat over the boy's shoulders and ruffled his hair. 'Well let's go then cowboy. Looks like we have some adventures to be getting on with.' The boy smiled half-heartedly, and Jack tried to smile back. He put his hand on the boy's shoulder and they walked back the way they had come the day before, toward the mountains, and the coming storm.

TWENTY-FIVE

Rogers couldn't sleep. With Maria's bullet proof drapes gone, the orange city lights were having a field day. It was like sleeping in an incubator. His thoughts drifted from Maria to another woman. The only other lady he'd ever lost. His fists clenched involuntarily as he thought about that day for the first time in a long while. Dammit. A cold sweat broke out on his back. He thought about calling old Bob. His oldest friend. The man that had taken him in when he had nothing left. An image of his mother's empty shoe lying on the street flashed through his mind and he blanked it out. He'd become an expert at that recently. He reached for his cell and thumbed on the display. 5:03 a.m. Bob would be up now and cooking breakfast. An old habit. A souvenir from his days on the beat. Rogers' thumb scrolled down and hovered over Bob's landline number. What would he even say? 'Hey, I know it's been a while Bob, I've been too busy with my failing marriage to call, but now that she's left me I could do with the company'? He switched the phone off and dropped it onto the bed. The cell phone's screen lit up, lighting the ceiling. A slight pause and then the ringtone and vibration started up loudly. Rogers had wondered when the gloating would start. He'd expected her to make it through one night at least. He scooped it up and looked at the caller ID; Bob, Home. Shit, had he called him by accident? He clenched his eyes shut and thumbed the green icon.

'Bob? Did I wake you?'

A loud crackle cut across him. '10-13 Connor. I have only 30 seconds here. I see them coming. Do you still have it?' Bob's voice, firm, strong, determined.

Rogers sat up immediately. 10-13. Officer needing assistance. Then two things happened. Three sharp knocks on the front door, and the phone line went dead on Bob's side, leaving his words hanging in the air. Rogers jumped out of bed, threw open his sock drawer and felt around for his personal weapon. For a crazy second he thought Maria might have taken that too, but his fingers brushed against the cold steel right at the back. He unclipped the empty magazine and dropped it onto the bed. Fished in the drawer beneath, found the two full clips. Butted one into its place, heard the click-click, and shoved the other into his briefs against the small of his back. He made sure the safety was off, ratcheted a round into the chamber and thumbed back the trigger. He unscrewed the bulb in his bedroom. He walked quickly to the living area, unscrewed the main bulb there too. If they were amateurs they would flick on the lights. They would be confused by the darkness for a second or two. Would maybe try the switch again – an automatic human response to a blown lightbulb – try it again. By the time they did, they would be dead. He strode silently to the front door and crouched low and listened. Not a sound came from the other side. He placed both bulbs on the floor - another makeshift distraction. When a person makes a noise when he's trying to be quiet, he freezes for a second. It's the shock of the noise coupled with trying to be absolutely silent to compensate. Again, it's hardwired into the human condition. Can't be unlearned without training. It isn't a long paralysis, but long enough. He walked quickly to the opposite end of the room, picking up the black book from the fruit bowl as he did. He switched off their ancient refrigerator to disable the automatic light mechanism, opened its polished steel door and used it as a shield between him and the front door. Then he waited. And hoped they were amateurs.

They were pros. The knock at the door was nothing but a decoy. They came in through the bedroom window. And they came in fast and hard. Rogers heard a single sharp blow shatter the large pane of toughened glass into a thousand pieces. Rogers had done it himself a hundred times in many situations. A single hard tap in the top-right corner. Then he heard a soft double thud. It sounded to Rogers a lot like a 200lb man in full combat gear landing into a crouch position on his carpeted bedroom floor. Shit. Now his cover was useless. It was only good against a front entry. From the side he might as well be wearing a target on his chest. He quickly left his position and skirted around to the other side of the table and pushed himself low and prone into the corner, facing the bedroom entrance. The window above and behind him would make him invisible at least for an instant, even if they had night vision. The cat mewled with curiosity and joined him on the floor. Not now. He gave her a prod and she fled off into the darkness. Rogers breathed slow and steady. Aimed just below the centre of the bedroom doorknob. Just below waist height. Just below the point a kevlar vest stops being effective. The doorknob turned. Rogers held the gun steady, and fired.

TWENTY-SIX

'So what have we got?' The surgeon yawned and walked through the interior double doors, almost dancing around a bored looking night-porter. The surgeon's colleague, a portly man, jogged to keep up with him. He handed him a report including some injury photographs. The surgeon ignored them. His colleague continued regardless.

'It's not pretty. Found him waist deep in mud. Legs are shot to shit. Looks like some sort of prolonged torture. He's got multiple foreign bodies in his legs, bones are all crushed, skin is flayed. Major arteries ripped to shreds. I don't know how he's still alive. He should have bled out long ago.'

'Have we stabilised him?'

'We've prepped him. They should be wheeling him into theatre right now.'

'Good.'

Then the lights went out. The ward was thrown into complete darkness. A woman's scream, a few groans and a clattering of a bedpan, then the generators kicked in and the lights came on one by one.

'Well that was fun.' The surgeon barely slowed and pushed on through the corridor. A woman in green coveralls came tumbling around the corner, her sneakers squeaking with every step.

'He's gone.'

'Too bad. Looks like you woke me for nothing then.' The surgeon stopped to take a mouthful of his warm coffee.

'No!' she screamed, making him jump. 'He didn't die. He's just gone!' She blurted out the rest in a continuous train. 'We were strapping his legs in for the procedure and the lights went out. They were out for only a second but when they came back... it's just empty. The bed's just fucking empty!' Then she ran back the way she came. The surgeon walked on quietly after her, studying the pictures in his hand as he went. Looking back at him from the page was an African American male he didn't recognise, just another John Doe, with only the whites of his eyes looking out at him.

'Gotta love the night shift.' He smiled at his colleague and handed back the now unnecessary report. His colleague shivered and glanced down at the front page. He looked at the eyes in particular. He shivered. *Spooky*. He didn't know it but he was looking into the eyes of the future President of the USA, Captain Benjamin Freeman.

TWENTY-SEVEN

The ancient man sat silently, his eyes closed. Thinking. Akuti's heart thumped in her chest. She had spoken for several minutes, telling the Grey Wolf every detail of what she had seen by the ocean. He had listened to her without interruption, with only the momentarily widening of his eyes any indication at all that he was hearing her words. After she had finished he blew out a long, deep breath and closed his eyes. His second face had remained impassive throughout her visit but now it watched her with a curious glint in its malformed eye. Akuti wondered if Grey Wolf believed her. Certainly, she had begun to doubt herself. She had been certain at the time that what she had seen was indeed the great prophecy of her childhood - the Great Buffalo's arrival. She had seen the powerful warriors overcome by the spirit God and finally had watched as he had made himself invisible and reappeared a moment later from the spirit world, speaking with an unearthly tongue. She had used this last event as a distraction to make her retreat unseen. She did not know what became of the Buffalo after that, but her faithful horse had been fleet of foot and she knew Grey Wolf would know how to track him down. She remembered well the old legend and hoped that now, their own spirit god, the great Coyote, could soon return to the stars and reward them well.

The ancient man's eyes opened, and he smiled. He held out his hand to Akuti, and spoke firmly.

"You have done well but there is much to do now. Let us gather the elders."

The old man rose unsteadily and winced. He gripped his bad arm, clenching his eyes shut while the pain took hold. Akuti had never known the old man to be free of pain. It seemed to be an affliction that had always ailed him. He had strong medicines, crushed powders of many plants, that helped keep the painful demons away, but they never truly left him alone. His second face seemed to be his blessing and his curse. Akuti watched as he shook off the spasm and for the first time she saw him smile.

"I have lived for so long with this agony that it has become my closest friend. But even the closest companions can sometimes become enemies. Now, come, we must prepare."

TWENTY-EIGHT

The gunshot was deafening in the darkness. The muzzle flash left a freeze-frame of the kitchen in Rogers's mind. He saw the bedroom door splinter about half way down as his bullet tore through. He threw himself as far as he could to the right. If he had missed, the return fire would be immediate. There was nothing. No sound except the whistling in his ears. He forced his breathing to slow, and waited, his gun held steadily with both hands in front of him, his right finger tense on the trigger. He waited. Thin slivers of orange light pierced through the gaps in the bedroom door. The strips of dim light were unwavering and constant. Nothing moved on the other side. He slowly got up to a standing position when a dark shape burst from the shadows on his left and filled his field of vision. He jerked the gun clumsily toward the intruder and his finger squeezed the trigger to within a fraction of releasing the hammer. He exhaled quickly as he realised how close he had come to shooting George. George hissed and fled toward his usual safety zone of the bedroom. *Georgina, no.* The cat's nose had barely touched the gap between door and frame when the whole door erupted into blue-white flames, disintegrating the animal and the thick wooden panel into white-hot dust.

What the hell?

Rogers crouched down hard, and emptied the entire clip through the black doorway. The gun's thunder roaring over and over in the small room. He heard a ricochet and a shout accompany his third shot, but it was quickly drowned out by his fourth and fifth. He let the empty clip clatter onto the kitchen floor, clicking the second magazine home immediately in its place. Thick grey smoke made visibility impossible. Rogers skirted the oak table by memory alone, never taking his eyes away from the black hole of the bedroom doorway. What had happened to the street lights? With the door gone, the room should have been brighter now, not darker. What the hell had they used? That was like no explosion he'd ever seen. He pushed the thoughts of his wife's cat to the back of the queue. There would be a time for that later. A breeze blew in from the bedroom, clearing the smoke a little. Rogers blinked and tensed as he saw some movement in the far corner. He approached with caution, pausing in-between steps to re-aim and re-evaluate. His hand went automatically to a radio that wasn't there.

Backup was a luxury he didn't have this time. His hand brushed instead against the black book shoved into his brief's waistband. The damned book. The book had been his comfort blanket for many years. It was the only thing he had left of her. Now it looked like it was going to get him killed. Whoever wanted it and for whatever reason, they didn't seem to be fucking about. Bob had always warned him about today. And together they had prepared as best as they could about what they would need to do. Connor thought their plan might still work too, if only he got through the next thirty seconds without being turned into a human firecracker.

The bedroom was still. No movement, no light, nothing. Only a steady breeze that filled the room with a strange combined aroma of burned cinders and pine trees. He grabbed an empty beer bottle from the counter and lobbed it with an underarm swing into the bedroom. It disappeared into the blackness and he heard nothing but a muted thud as it landed. There was no gunfire, no explosions, no spontaneous combustion. Things were looking up. Perhaps one of his bullets had hit their target after all. He grabbed another, threw it harder, hoping to break it against the bedroom's back wall. Maybe wake up any stunned assailants on the other side, make them jump, make a sound, anything. The bottle didn't break. It only travelled further and made the same thud, just further away. Which was impossible. Rogers knew how deep the room was. He knew the bottle should have hit that wall a full two seconds before it had actually landed. Just what in the hell was going on here? Had they blown through the far wall too with that explosion? He shook his head and blinked the smoke away. He couldn't rule out the possibility that he was concussed. He could still hear the ringing in his ears. He tried to breath a little slower, calm himself down. His palms were slick, and his trigger finger trembled a little too much. Whoever was in his house was no ordinary intruder, but they were still intruders, and was damned if he'd let any man just walk into his home and leave without letting Rogers introduce himself properly. George had always been a pain in the ass, but she had still been a faithful pain in the ass. This last thought fired up his adrenaline again, and his anger overpowered his fear. He strode deliberately into the bedroom and fired four covering shots, moving from high to low, left to right, and finishing in a low crouch, with the next two bullets primed for the first visible movement. There was nothing. Rogers blinked as the smoke cleared. His bare feet touched not carpet, but something cooler. It reminded him of an early morning visit to the Hamptons as a child. The sand had been cool underfoot. The breeze seemed stronger now, and he glanced at the window instinctively, looking for the city lights. Rogers mouth dropped open, and he dropped his guard, the intruder forgotten. The window wasn't there. the wall wasn't there either. There were no walls. He craned his neck back and looked up to a ceiling that wasn't there either. He could see moonlight creeping through thin gaps in a patch of cloudy sky. Jesus, what the hell was this. It wasn't just as if the walls had been destroyed, it was more like he had walked out of the building. All around him trees and shrubbery grew. If there had been more light he was sure that he would see the same for miles around.

There were no city lights, only darkness outside. But wasn't he already outside? He looked down at his feet, and saw that he was standing on dark earth. Blades of grass sprouted through the soil here and there, tickling his toes. It was if he had stepped into an open woodland instead of a six foot box room. Never mind that he was on the second floor. He had a flash of vertigo and wheeled around to grab hold of the doorframe. The unreal sight of his kitchen illuminated by moonlight only added to the nausea and he closed his eyes to steady himself. The door frame was ice cold to the touch, and he wondered again about the explosion. He heard something crack out in the distance and he regained his composure, the threat of the intruder crashing back to the front of his mind. He moved quickly. He ran back into the kitchen, grabbed and stepped into his old jogging pants from George's bed, snatched an old NYPD hooded sweater from the counter, and took his belt from the chair. He slipped on a pair of black sneakers and took a moment to tie them properly, keeping one eye on the bedroom doorway as he did so. It would do no good to trip over his own laces in there for the sake of getting a two second head start. He took out his service revolver, loaded it, then checked the safety. The weight felt good in his hand. He shoved the black book into the empty holster, and jammed his personal piece in behind it. He rooted behind the pantry door, and found two more full clips of ammo. Shoved them into a spare pouch on the belt, and headed for the door. He clicked on his maglite and twisted the beam to spotlight mode. Then he clicked it off and held it as a brace for his gun hand. Torch and weapon facing ahead as standard procedure, left hand ready to switch on the light, right hand ready to fire the gun. Then without looking back, he stepped through what had once been the bedroom door, into the unknown.

TWENTY-NINE

Freeman's mind had no clarity. He could only see in flashes. He didn't know if they were memories or events that were happening at this moment. He only knew of the pain that came with them. He saw himself in a falling steel cage. Heard the hiss of air leave as the oxygen supply was compromised. Felt himself swim away into a fog, fighting against the sleep. The klaxons waking him as the craft drifted off course. Saw his own hand reach too late for the magnetic coil, the huge tidal waves almost licking the falling hull's glass belly by the time he pulled the cord, and then the crash of impact. Then darkness. He awoke again with his legs on fire, and rain in his eyes. Red and blue lights, a needle in his arm, a mask on his face. The world swam away but still the pain remained. When he came back the pain was greater, but so were his senses. His trained mind was already racing through his options. Survive first, reminisce later. He had no memory of who he was or how he got here. But he saw that he was in a medical facility, with people trying to fix him. No immediate threat. His legs were on fire, and he couldn't fight past the pain. He knew that no medical facilities could help him. He didn't know how he knew any of this, he just had a deep ingrained knowledge of what he needed to do to survive. He needed to give his mind and body some time, shut the pain off manually. It had been called a manual reset during training. It meant shutting the body down by activating the nano bots twice within a short period. By reactivating them while they were still in their recharge cycle they would enter their standby phase. Essentially they would power down all of their host's non essential biological systems , giving them the resources needed to heal their power source, the host body. There were a couple of side effects. One being an incremental time jump of a few seconds. The main by-product was of course that the host body would be completely shut down. An induced coma.

He had little power in his hands, and his legs were no use, but he could just about focus past the fog long enough to squeeze his jaw shut. His last coherent thought before the darkness took him was one of abstract wonder. The lights above his bed were dancing.

With the sudden increase in jaw pressure, the blood from Freeman's tender gums trickled onto his tongue. The dormant artificial cells reacted instantly with the saliva in his mouth, the first catalyst for digestion, and the nano-bots ignited in a chain reaction through his body. His bloodstream became a wave of silent re-boot instructions. Each micro-synthetic capsule signalling its neighbour to enter the shutdown phase. His blood pumped through his body, carrying the message along his arteries, through his veins and into tiny capillaries. The cells travelled unseen along connected IV lines, and through tiny pores in the electrical sensors on his chest. The nano-bots went into hibernation with a huge surge of negative ion energy, plunging the hospital into darkness and flickering Ben Freeman briefly out of existence.

THIRTY

They could smell the carnage before they saw it. The thick black smoke greeted them over the final ridge. There was no barking to welcome them this time, only a grim silence. The boy saw the smouldering ruin and slipped from Jack's grip. He ran towards his home, screaming the dog's name. Jack cursed and ran after him. The old man had told him what to expect but his instinct was still to protect the boy. He caught up to little Sonny just as he reached the charred grassland. A blackened post jutted out of the ground, still crackling with red embers at its tip. The dog's wooden post. The mutt's last stand. Jack knelt down and held the screaming boy close. He buried the boy's face into his chest, sparing him the prolonged sight of the charred fist-sized skull on the ground. The boy pushed Jack away and Jack saw the farmhouse's fire burn in the boy's wet eyes. Jack saw the boy become a man in that instant. The last trails of childhood burned away forever. He looked up at Jack.

'They will die where they stand. The bastards will die a thousand deaths.'

Jack's sweat suddenly felt cold with the realisation that this was the moment the boy's journey began. If he meant it or not, the boy would likely have the opportunity to fulfil his vengeful promise to the letter.

Jack looked to the sky for answers that weren't there. He had his own errands to run. Where he was going was no place for the boy. He planned to stop the devil himself and there had already been one too many lives lost on that particular journey. The black book dug into his flesh as he moved and reminded him of even more complications. He watched the boy wipe away his tears and the loss Jack saw in those eyes reminded him so much of another boy, many years gone. The boy's face darkened.

'Where's Pa? You don't think...' The boy looked suddenly terrified.

'No.' Jack put a quick stop to such thoughts. He sighed and pushed himself up, adjusting his hat against the early sun. 'I have an idea about your Pa's whereabouts, and if I'm right, then he's far, far away from here.'

The boy calmed a little.

'Come. Let's see if we can't track down these bastards and bring hell to their door, what do you say?'

The boy, realising he was no longer an army of one, blushed with gratitude.

Jack held out his hand; A gesture of support.

'Walk with me son. Let me show you something.'

They walked together toward the burning shell of the house. The old man had been right. It was all gone. Burned to the ground. A cooking pot and some old iron tool were the only survivors inside the wooden carcass. The solid wooden table and stools nothing but stumps of black charcoal. It had been a furnace. Jack walked the perimeter with the boy, kicking the smoking earth as he went, searching for something. The boy looked up at Jack for the first few steps, hoping for answers. Jack ignored him and stuck to the task. The boy gave up eventually and held his eyes on the ground too, his grubby feet mimicking Jack's boots, overturning stones, pushing through thick black knots of grass.

It was the boy that eventually found it, and Jack was glad. It would help a little with the boy's healing. Not much, but something that would at least help him focus his anger. The boy held up the item with curiosity. When he realised what it was he trembled. He brimmed with anger at what they had done and a great pride that the dog had gone down fighting. It was an index finger, chewed off at the bone. It was dark with soot, but not burned. Two more lay close by, and a thumb. The boy picked them up as if they were precious stones. He held them up to show Jack, but would not hand them over completely. Jack offered no objection. The boy would have his spoils of war. Besides, Jack had already learned all he needed from the first glance. He had an idea where he could find the owner of the digits, and that would lead to some answers. For the boy's sake and for his. Someone had tried to kill him last night, and Jack had never been one to forgive easily.

THIRTY-ONE

The hospital lights flickered back on and the patient was gone. A female member of staff screamed in surprise, and stumbled backward over the instruments trolley. Another ran out of the double doors. The anaesthetist was closest to the patient when it happened and was the only one that saw what happened next. He had time to notice the IV drip that lay disconnected across the bedsheets. The cardiac monitor cables slithered off the bed, pulled down by their own weight. He saw the pink blood-soaked gown lying forgotten on top of the bed linen. The sheets themselves now covered in caked dark mud, stones, rusty nails, and random fragments of glass and steel. It looked like someone had emptied a bucket of debris onto the bed. There was a moment of calm, then he saw the patient flicker back into existence on the bed. Like strobe lighting at a disco. Somewhere outside he heard shouting, and sneakers making a u-turn back towards the theatre. He just stood there, unable to react, studying the naked patient. The patient seemed to be breathing regularly, curled into an extreme foetal position. The anaesthetist saw that the man's bleeding had stopped. A dark crust of blood had congealed at the corner of his mouth, and his crushed legs were a criss cross of thick pink scars. While the bed sheets and gown still dripped with a ruby-red shine, all the blood on the man's wounds were dark and dry. They looked like they had healed. The anaesthetist's mind finally succumbed to this new reality and he gripped the bed frame for support as his legs gave way under him. He heard the staff burst into the room, their bewildered shouts muffled by the roar of blood in his ears. His final thought as he fainted was of the blinking red light on the ceiling. He watched the hypnotic red light as the rest of the world turned into a thick haze.

The tiny light emitting diode was attached to the front of a black and chrome device about the size of a small penlight. It was housed in a clear glass dome. It had a wide angle aperture and was surrounded by a cluster of 8 infra red LEDs. The device was a standard night vision closed circuit camera installed in most of the new medical units. It silently transmitted the unfolding events as packets of zeros and ones to an offsite, unmonitored secure server almost four hundred miles away.

THIRTY-TWO

The scratching was getting worse. His mind was a dark fog. He'd been in this glass box all his life and his mind was the only company he had known for a long, long time. The scratching was an intrusion. It made him angry. The light patterns streaming in to the life support unit were changing. Weeds now blocked out most of the sunlight that seeped into the outer room.

It had once been brighter. Much brighter. He remembered artificial lights. Moving shapes he knew to be his protectors. They had talked to him through the glass. Their voices had been comforting. Their instruments and tools had sparkled under the lights. Then they had stopped coming. They had left him all alone. For years he had been here. *And now this scratching*. His body felt warm and he felt an urge to change things. He had never felt the urge to move in all the years he was entombed. His mind could always go wherever it needed without any need for the weak vessel it lived inside. *But the scratching.* He would stop that scratching and the world would be calm again.

His mind told his arm to move up and it did so. His eyes saw the arm float up into view. The life fluid around him swirled and the outside world bobbed out of focus. He bought his other hand up to his face and he looked upon his own hands. They seemed larger now. He had been growing in here. He clenched his fists and thrust them outwards. They hit the glass wall and he felt pain for the first time. His mouth drew into a smile. This was a new feeling. He would like to feel that again. He pushed against the glass with more strength and felt his bones click and twist under the pressure. He gave out a wet yelp of delight. Bracing his back against the far side of his chamber he pushed the front wall of glass away from him until the blood in his ears roared. A tiny crack appeared in the center, and he exhaled sharply. Bubbles from his mouth warped his vision and he forced himself to become calm. He traced the crack with a long bony finger, his nail finding the groove and snaking down until it reached the widest point. With new vigor he lashed out at the crack, hitting it twice, three times, and then a fourth. Tiny bubbles of air now rose up from several places and he targeted those places with a final flurry of punches. The glass gave way and the crack grew into a gaping mouth and shattered the glass plate into a thousand tiny pieces.

The liquid surged out onto the cold concrete floor and the life form inside collapsed under its own weight inside the suddenly empty steel tank. It choked on the cold air and retched and gagged until its insides burned. What had he done? He couldn't see, he couldn't breathe and he couldn't think. *That terrible scratching still clawed at his mind.* He used the steel framework of the pod and hauled himself out, flopping onto the wet laboratory floor like a newly born calf. He blinked and saw the brightest source of pain. A bright wall of glass. Weeds poked through in places and the sun burned brightly on the other side of it, mocking him. *The scratching noise was all around him.* He dragged his weak form toward the sunlight, suddenly overwhelmed with rage. He would squeeze the life out of the white ball of pain. The room buckled and darkened as he willed his muscles to pull him onward. He saw bright purple stars and then there were only dreams.

THIRTY-THREE

The old man stood and watched as they slept. The stars faded briefly as the wind pushed the clouds overhead. One last flame danced on the fire, throwing an orange flicker over Jack and the boy. Sonny saw that they were both uneasy in their sleep. He crept away as quietly as he could, the last ember giving out, leaving only the smell of smoke on his clothes. He wished he could stay a while longer. He knew only too well that the boy would not take it well, and would carry it with him for the rest of his days. Even now, knowing why it had to happen, old Sonny couldn't quite put that loss behind him. Tears rolled down the cracks of his cheeks and yet he smiled as he walked on toward the mountains. He had come full circle in life, and soon he would be out of the loop forever, with the boy taking his place at the start. But first he had someone to see. He hadn't seen him in years. It would be a pleasure to see him again. *Yes sir*, a goddamned pleasure. Sonny's fists clenched involuntarily at the thought and he redoubled his pace. Somewhere in the darkness a fox screeched. And Sonny walked on.

THIRTY-FOUR

In the dream, Jack sees his daughter. That's how he knows he's dreaming.

His breathing quickens and he shakes his head. He tries to wake up but already knows that he won't until he sees it happen again. She giggles as she dances away from him. His legs are useless blocks of wood, his mouth full of tar. All he can do is bring his gun hand up and aim past her. Aim at whatever comes for her this time. The scenery moves past him as he ambles forward. It doesn't look real. The distant mountains are like theatre props, endlessly scrolling by on pull-ropes and winches. He is a cardboard mannequin, destined to move too slowly through the screeching winds. He can hear her laughter for a few seconds more, then there is only the wind. His face feels warm. There is a vocal rumbling sound. It's almost a groan. It's faint, but he can hear it. He always hears it.

Then she comes. Ahead, through the dark tunnel of his vision, she comes toward him. *The Witchen.* She's horrifically tall. Much taller than he is. Her head bowed down low, her stick legs and bone arms sticking out from beneath the long burlap sack. Her hair blows like oiled straw in the wind and she shimmers, as if she were nothing but a swarm of black bees. He sees her head begin to lift from her chest and he knows that if their eyes meet it will be the end of him.

He raises his gun higher and sees that it is not loaded. It has no chambers to fill. It is a gun of dreams - only a metaphor. Jack knows that metaphors don't need bullets. He pulls the trigger. The pistol barks four times. The witch's head erupts with each kick and roar. Black flesh rips away from the skull, revealing the dark bone of something that is far from human. He empties the gun into the skull, shattering it into pieces. The fragments float on the wind and become a single pitch-black butterfly of death. The witch creeps on toward him without her head. He shoots again.

The shots puncture her torso, her legs, and her arms. Long trails of blood drag on behind her and still she comes. She is almost upon him now and the stench of her is terrifying. It symbolizes all of his fears, all of his loss, bound in a bleeding wet blackness. He raises his hand inches away from where her head should be and focuses on something in the distance. He aims, closes his eyes, and shoots. The bullet flies true, piercing the void above her neck and tearing through the insect behind her – the black butterfly. As the moth explodes into oblivion, the witch crumbles at his feet and fades into wisps of charcoal ash.

Jack breathes out and continues on. He knows that she was only the first of many monstrosities. Every night he has the same dream, and every night he fails. He never saves his daughter. He knows he can't undo the past, but because he has no other choice, he grits his teeth against the howling wind, and he tries again.

THIRTY-FIVE

It was the dirt that Rogers felt first. He needed to take a leak and the damned dirt was in his shoes. There was warmth on his face and he awoke in the midday sun. He sat up and looked left and right. A black asphalt road ran as far as he could see in both directions. A fuzzy shimmer blurred the furthest points. His head felt like the day after his twenty-first all over again. With a groan he stood up and vomited. Jesus Christ. What the hell had he been drinking last night? Images flashed in his head but there was little time for that now. First things first - he stepped a couple of polite steps away from the road and relieved himself. It felt like he'd been holding it in forever. His thoughts went to the most pressing memories. His wife. Was that real? Was she gone? He would fix that. He had to. But then the rest of the evening crashed down on him. Christ. He placed a hand on his forehead. What kind of messed up shit was this? He remembered an intruder, something about being outside looking at the starry night sky with the cat. What the hell was he doing here? Where was he? He shielded his eyes against the light and saw a building about a mile down the road - a truck stop. He took off both his sneakers and emptied them onto the track. The small pile of sand was much darker in color than the road beneath and the world swam away from him briefly. He struggled to tie his laces and started the head-pounding journey toward the diner on the horizon. His hands patted down his pockets out of habit. And froze. His gun. He remembered slipping his gun into his pants. It was missing. He whirled around and checked his waistband frantically. Nothing. He strode back to the side of the road, the headache momentarily forgotten. He had nothing on him except his clothes and his shoes. No keys, no wallet, no gun, and no black book.

It was gone.

"Shit." He carefully traced his steps back to the exact spot that he had been laying when he came to. He saw his footprints make shuffling steps from a rounded bowl in the dirt. There were a few more footprints spaced further apart and leading toward it from a copse of trees some way from the road. He followed the prints, his heart beating harder. The footprints became lighter as the dry soil turned into knotted grassy streaks. In the shelter of the first lot of trees he found a rough opening leading into marshy woodland beyond. The footsteps stopped abruptly at the mouth, but a little further in he could make out wet indentations that were probably sunken footmarks. He took a last glance down the highway toward civilization and stepped into the darker coolness of the wetlands.

THIRTY-SIX

Akuti rode ahead of Old Gray Wolf. To their sides were two of the village's strongest and fastest -their protectors for the long road ahead. Akuti knew one as being their elder's personal protector, Taroo, who always travelled with him. The other, Kaaru, was a little younger than Akuti, and they had played together as children. He had shown great promise this past year with his huntsman skills.

Their horses trotted at a much slower pace than Akuti was comfortable with. The horses' movement was courteous to the elder of course; his pain must have been immeasurable with each stray footstep and jolt. Akuti glanced back and saw only a silent double mask of calm from the old man. She turned her attention back to the path ahead. They had left with the sunrise and had travelled far already, but at this rate she knew not if they would reach the beach by nightfall. Even if they did it would be a long night ahead whatever they found there. The young warrior Taroo suddenly screeched, mimicking the sound of a tree rat.

The party stopped instantly.

It was their warning signal. The horses harrumphed and shook their manes in protest, eager to move onwards. The young man who had raised the alarm slid off his horse and ran ahead softly, one hand clutching four arrows, the other gripping his bow. Kaaru steered his horse to the front, his weapons unsheathed, a human shield between the threat and the elder. Akuti maneuvered her horse silently to the side, to a stronger hillside position. And waited. The old man seemed unmoved by any of these events and simply waited for the moment to pass. Several long minutes went by. No irregular noise or movements alerted Akuti to any kind of danger but something was firing her instincts to run. She wanted to bolt, to kick her horse's flank and to get as far away as possible, but she fought the feeling, mistaking those thoughts for weakness. She edged further up the hillside instead, where she could better see her group and any danger that might come from the woods. And then it came in one terrible instant.

Two arrows flew silently from within the trees. The first found nothing but air - the air warmed by Akuti's breath only a moment earlier. The second flew straight and entered Kaaru's skull through his right eye socket. He tumbled off his horse and slipped quietly into the tall grass, and then the silence was shattered. Akuti's horse cried out in surprise and Kaaru's mare bolted. Grey Wolf's ride sprang into life too, throwing the old man to the ground. Akuti heard him cry out in pain. She watched as the three rider-less horses kicked and bucked their way out of the clearing and away from the commotion. She acted quickly, out of instinct and training, not with any conscious thoughts. Tapping her horse's sides quickly with her heels, she ducked her head low behind the cover of the muscular neck. The horse galloped toward the fallen old man. Akuti was there in moments, dropping to the ground by his side. She saw that he was not awake. She slapped the rump of her horse and yelled the command for him to flee. Alone in the tall grass, she was all that stood between the attackers and the Grey Wolf. She had to assume the worst, that Taroo had also been hurt or killed. A solitary scream came from the woods and a human shape rushed toward them through the grass. Akuti's hairs stood on end as she prepared to fight to her death to protect the elder. The attacker was a monstrosity, drenched in blood from the head down, and shouting her name. He slowed a few steps away and fell awkwardly to his knees. She saw that the blood was not his own and he was unarmed. It was Taroo.

"Akuti, we are safe, they are no more." and with that he fell exhausted onto his back, his breath a ragged loop and his eyes rolling back almost to their whites in their sockets.

THIRTY-SEVEN

The creature awakens. He does not know how much time has passed but the sunlight has gone. *The scratching in his head is as loud as ever.* He pushes himself up onto his knees and the world bends away briefly. He grips a solid surface for balance and hauls himself upright. His balance settles after some moments and he realizes that the air does not burn him any more. He is breathing air. He shuffles towards the glass window and sees only darkness on the other side. The scratching in his head makes it difficult for him to think about anything. A curious tiny winged animal lands on the window ledge and stands there, chirping, adjusting its head position erratically, and studying every movement the creature makes.

The bird's arrival has made the scratching louder, and the creature's instincts move his body before his consciousness realizes it. His hand shoots out, snatching the bird in its stained claws in a fraction of a moment between two heartbeats. The bird opens and closes its beak silently in shock. The creature brings the bird closer to his own face to investigate. It can feel the vibration of its blood flow and the fluttering of its tiny organs. The creature loses interest and crushes the bird without a further thought. More interesting to him than the blood trickling down his forearm and the sudden cessation of warmth within the tiny animal is the sudden silence.

There is no scratching.

He wonders if it was the bird that was making the scratching noise. He grins and lets the bird drop to the wet floor. He can think clearly again and thinks of all the sensations he has yet to try with his new found freedom. He likes the sight of the darkness outside the window and believes he would like to go there next. He moves toward the window, a little more gracefully now, his inquisitive mind hungry for more sensations, the bird's crushed remains already long forgotten.

THIRTY-EIGHT

The sunlight fell diagonally across Freeman's lap as he gazed out across the lawn. The window was a large one, allowing a broad view of the outside world, but the bars on it were far from decorative. President Benjamin Freeman scratched at a lazy beard he had acquired these past few weeks and yawned. He wheeled the chair a little closer so that he could follow a sparrow's path below the window ledge. To the onlooker he would appear disheveled and impassive, but Freeman's mind was running at full capacity. He looked up from the hopping bird to the long grass strip, past the morning patrol and to the trees at the far end. He saw the tall arching chain link fence, and the five lengths of electrical wire running across the stretch of blank space at the top. He saw the lone guard with the big bear of a dog exchange pleasantries with the afternoon shift as they hopped off their buggy. The military medical institution's left wing stretched for almost an acre toward the front gate and ran perpendicularly to the older structure of the main building.

There was a subtle settling of a floor panel on the inside of the room's locked entrance, and the room's temperature seemed to drop by a couple of degrees.

Freeman willed himself to breathe normally and continue exploring the world outside his new prison. Behind him, by the doorway, a tall man in a fitted dark suit licked his lips. His skin seemed to ripple as he did so.

"I'm not sure why anyone would break into a high security establishment, or what tricks you keep pulling to do so but I'm sure your reasons are well worth taking the time from a busy morning to listen to them." Freeman spoke without taking his eyes from the window.

The creature behind him smiled, and he remained by the shadow of the grand old archway. The sunlight seemed not to reach him there.

"You intrigue me chief. You certainly do. To put yourself through so much trouble, just to get yourself stranded here. Do you wonder sometimes what part in this madness is yours? What pitiful jigsaw piece you'll become?" the creature scratched a face that looked older than sand.

Freeman held his composure and tried to hear above the screaming of his heartbeat. This past week he had reached the conclusion that he had either truly gone mad and this recurring apparition was a symptom of his condition, or worse... that he hadn't.

"What part do *you* play, would you say, if you'll forgive me my curiosity?" Freeman wished that he could use his damned legs so that he wouldn't have to take this craziness sitting down like a duck in a skeet shoot. He was just about ready for a fistfight - anything except these off-kilter mind games. Sweat poured down his back now, soaking his undershirt and he forced himself to look for the sparrow - to seek out calmness in this crazy mess. A loud mechanical sound behind him made him flinch visibly in his chair and he cursed his nerves for allowing such a weakness to overcome him. He whipped round to look his cursed apparition in the eyes, but instead saw only a white suited orderly, opening up the secure door and whistling as he entered the room. There was no one else. Freeman exhaled. As the orderly carried in a fresh bedpan and clattered about his menial tasks, the President glanced out again at the calm scene outside. His eye line traced the sparrow's footprints in the damp grass, untouched yet by the morning sunlight, and stopped when he found the little bird in the shadows. It was lying on its side, its tiny beak opening and closing in a slow, fragile rhythm. He'd seen it a few times before. Birds caught by a cat or having mistaken a closed window for an open one. Birds in deep traumatic shock. *Dying.* Freeman shivered. He had to get moving. Away from this madness. It was time to bring the plan forward.

THIRTY-NINE

Jack and the boy reached a large rocky outcrop at around midday. The sun was bright and warm and they were both silent. Jack scoured the valley below for any sign of movement. Little Sonny kicked at the dust with his boots. Jack swiped at a fly that took an interest in his moist forehead and took a moment to catch his breath. Below them, over the edge of the cliff, stretched a green tree belt of several acres. In the distance they could hear the promise of water. Jack shook his makeshift canteen and heard a last mouthful sloshing about in the container.

"Here, boy." He offered out his hand. Sonny took the pouch and drank gladly. He offered the drained jug back to Jack. Jack shook his head. "You keep it son. If you're man enough to drink a man's last drink, you're man enough to carry its weight." Sonny looked down, unsure if he was being reprimanded.

Jack's sneaky smile told him otherwise and the boy's frown faded.

"Thank you."

Jack thought the boy needed a boost. He had no idea where old Sonny Senior had gone, or how to find him. He would have to do the only other thing he could for now and that was to keep the boy's mind occupied.

"Say, do you hear the river down that gulley?" Jack pointed over the edge. "That's where we need to be before nightfall. I think that's a fine place for a couple of tired travelers to set up camp for the night, wouldn't you think?"

The boy's face darkened. Jack realized again that little Sonny was nothing but a scared child, forced into a man's world too soon. It scared him how quickly he could forget. How naturally he himself could absorb life's heaviness and assume that others did the same.

"Pa won't be there. He will be waiting for us someplace else. What if those men have him?"

"Steady now son. Your pa has other things to tend to. His path doesn't cross with those men. He already knew of their intention and told me so the night before he… the night he went on his own track. He was always one step ahead of those fools."

The boy seemed to think this through. "He's not like us is he? Pa I mean. He's different."

Jack took a breath and scanned the horizon for answers. Or just for strength. *Where the hell was a whiskey when he needed one?* He hadn't done any parenting for a long while and this was an old and difficult road for him. He turned and crouched down next to the kid. He patted the ground with his hand, gesturing the boy to sit next to him. Sonny did so, with a sigh.

"Your father, the man you call pa, is a man who would do anything for his boy, you hear? We'll find him son, and then you can ask him all the damned questions you need to. But until then, we've only got each other to muddle through this and it's apt to be difficult enough as it is without second guessing about the things we have no answers for."

The boy dropped his head and scratched at the ground with a stick. The boy was lost. Jack could see that. The boy likely had years of questions just boiling at the surface, now that he had someone else to share them with. Jack remembered how old Sonny had always treated the boy as an equal. Jack exhaled before looking the boy in the eye.

"Your pa is different, that much you're right about. He knows things before they happen. It's because he's been there before, in a way. We'll talk more about this someday if we still find ourselves running in the same company, but for now, you can rest a little easier knowing that your pa isn't just another pa. He's special. And that's why I have an idea that he's safe, and doing something important that needs to be done."

Little Sonny sniffed and seemed to nod to himself. "I knew it. I sometimes thought it's because I'm small and he's old. But it's not that."

Jack smiled. "You're a clever boy, Sonny. Your Pa was right about that too. What do you say we find ourselves a camp for the night and find us some water to get rid of this mouth full of dust we seem to be carrying around with us? And maybe tomorrow, we'll be a step closer to your Pa."

The boy was already on his feet. He wiped the dirt from his pants with an absent minded slap of his little palms, and walked toward the steep drop. Jack marveled at the child's complete lack of fear and shuddered. That would help the boy hold on to his sanity with some of what was to come.

The boy turned, as if he was remembering something.

"Pa can wait. Tomorrow we have men to catch. You promised." And with that he clambered over the rim, leaving Jack feeling small and old and thirsty on the dusty cliff edge.

FORTY

The river was almost filled to bursting and Jack wondered about flooding. There hadn't been too much rain lately so there was no easy explanation for the swelling. Settlers maybe, or some natural obstruction down-river. He forced it to the back of his mind and went about preparing the fire. Little Sonny had already wandered off to fetch a second helping of driftwood and Jack didn't want the boy to see him pondering. They had chosen a spot on some high ground, in a clearing away from the water's edge. The nearest steady pool was hundreds of yards away and nothing but churning water ran past their camp. This was safest, so that no animals or passers by stumbled across them while looking for drinking water. Jack collected an armful of dried up hunks of wood and dropped them onto the pile. The boy returned with a smaller armful and blew out dramatically. Jack chuckled.

"Am I working you too hard there son?"

"There's just no easy firewood. It's either wet or still growing out of the ground. This is all there is." Sonny wiped a dirty sleeve along his mouth. Jack could see that keeping the boy busy was keeping him from thinking about too may questions, which was alright with him.

"Come here boy. Let me show you an old soldier's trick." Jack made a big show of scratching his head as if deep in thought and then looking carefully along the tree line in all directions before settling on a patch of trees he'd spotted previously to the East. "There. See those trees with the brown ferns all blackened by their base? I think you'll find what you're looking for somewhere around there."

The boy's brows dropped down over his eyes in exaggerated disbelief and he trudged there shaking his head. At first he just made a show of looking, kicking at the undergrowth, before shouting back.

"Nothing much here. Just some burnt grass."

"That just means you're in the right spot. Look properly now. Heed what I say." Jack assembled the smallest pieces of kindling into a reasonable version of a campfire and left the wet logs to dry on higher ground. The boy's shrill cry caught him off guard and his heart sprang in his chest.

"Wahoo! There's enough for a bonfire here." The boy was dragging half burnt chunks of timber longer than his arms from under the bushes. He was getting scratched and cut to hell doing so, but from the smile on his face Jack didn't think he was overly concerned.

"Well done son. Now, hush the hollering. Or everyone will be here stealing your plunder."

They dragged over a healthy amount of wood together before deciding that they had more than enough for two whole nights if needed, although Jack had long decided that they would have to leave again by daybreak. Whoever had left their stock of firewood would be back soon, and the river was already higher now than it had been when they arrived. Something wasn't right. It was best to be gone before any more distractions cropped up.

FORTY-ONE

The last of the alarms were shut down manually, one by one. The space station finally became quiet again. Smoke still drifted up from the wet launch room floor and seeped in through the cracks in the gallery overlooking the scene. The man in the pneumatic chair reversed away from the blacked out window and with his head slumped, left the room. His assistant took one last look at the charred room below and followed him out.

It took him almost thirty seconds to catch up with his boss. The chair was a sport version. His boss had never been shy of a little adrenaline.

"How is he? Any news?" The old man's voice was strong and calm, and he spoke without slowing down or turning around. The dark corridor added to the effect that his boss was simply a young man trapped in an old body. His assistant struggled to keep his own voice calm and keep the pace.

"He'll live. The shot was a little higher than expected but the medics were on site. The squib detonated perfectly and the Kevlar composite absorbed the impact as designed."

"Good. Let them know we're coming. He'll need to be de-briefed. As will the B-Team. And call the Ox's superiors. Officially, we'll have to inform them of his mutiny."

"But sir, the man is a hero. Surely…"

"They don't know that. Hell, we're not even supposed to know that yet. Assemble the relevant personnel and have them ready for me would you?"

"Yes sir. Of course."

The custom built wheel chair took the corner at its full velocity, and almost banked rather than turn into the second leg of its short journey. The suited assistant took that as his queue to drop back and slowed to a walk, flipping out his communicator and dialing in all the staff required for the next few meetings.

He watched the chair motor on down the grey hall, silhouetted against the bright ceiling lights at every ten feet. He shook his head in admiration. Some men seemed born for this job. He wished he had the same strength and stomach.

The gunmetal black chair stopped by an elevator door, and the old man's gnarled hand pressed the access button built into the chair's armrest. An infrared signal pinged the elevator's control panel and the light turned from amber to yellow. The sound of the descending cage vibrated the whole section of hallway, and the chair rolled back a fraction despite being in park mode. The old man blew out a long, tired breath and adjusted his collar.

The doors opened and he entered the elevator, closing the door remotely from his chair and using the voice command to signal the floor number.

"Medical bay. Lower base." The doors closed, and the elevator began its descent. The old man sat in silence and watched as the lights tracked up the elevator through the crack in the doors. The slither of orange reached the top of the doorway, then vanished before starting again at the bottom. A soft whoosh sound accompanied each passing light, and each one was quicker than the last. The elevator was designed to accelerate slightly with each floor it passed. By the time they approached the lower Medical floors, the light passed from floor to ceiling in under a second. The old man realized he'd been holding his breath and shook his head at his own irrational fear. The light slowed down to a crawl and the feeling passed. The doors opened with a deep guttural sound and the old man wheeled out into a sterile smelling light grey corridor. Security doors to his left and right prevented him from going any further without clearance. This particular floor had been especially cleared out for this occasion however and there was only one technician on the other end to allow entry, as requested. The old man rolled toward the doors on the left, and tapped a button on his chair. An electronic voice spoke over the intercom.

"Personnel, please identify for entry. Double clearance required for medical bay G23."

The old man tapped the security badge pinned on the inside of his dark jacket and spoke up.

"Freeman, Benjamin." He paused, before adding, "Retired."

After a few seconds, the porthole on the door opened and the General's face peered through. He smiled as he spoke. "General Jim Daniels here. Project leader. Security confirmed. Let him in."

The doors pushed open and out and Jim Daniels limped out to greet the new arrival. He winced and clutched his side as he did so, but smiled through the flash of pain.

"Well, well, well. You were right you crazy son of a bitch. Seems your trajectory memory may be a little off though," he said, patting his bandaged side.

The chair whirred from the darkness and the light from the medic-bay lit up old Freeman's frail face directly. The years had carved deep lines into his skin and his hair was mottled with tight pure white curls. A single streak of jet-black hair zigzagged from his temple to his ear - an anomaly of age, youthfulness refusing to let go.

Freeman smiled and scratched his chin with a liver-spotted right hand. His voice cracked a little. "I'm sorry about that Jim. I thought you might not go along with it if you knew exactly what a stubborn bastard I could be when I was younger."

"I've known you long enough for that." The General let out a chuckle and winced again, before raising his hand to signal he was okay. "It's like being winded, but with a sledgehammer. The doc says two broken ribs, which will heal fully by the end of the week if I keep the solution on it between bouts of saving the world."

Freeman laughed himself at this last. "We'd best get to it then. God knows what we've just started, and now all we have to do is see it through."

Freeman pressed the chair's control stick forward and whirred past the General, leaving him turning awkwardly on the spot and struggling to follow the old man's progress down the hall.

FORTY-TWO

Akuti ran through the scene in her mind in many different ways and then acted instantly. Her main focus was the old man. The others were only there to protect him after all, and to tend to them now would not be a logical step while the old man was hurt on the ground. She pulled him up off the floor to his knees, and was surprised at how heavy he was. He was out cold and a dead weight. Shelter was the first priority. They were vulnerable here, and a second attack would catch them off guard and unable to defend themselves. They had passed a large fallen tree only minutes previously. It was badly positioned across the path, and offered only minimal protection from most angles, but it was on slightly higher ground and within walking distance. It would have to do. She placed her right shoulder under Grey Wolf's armpit and used all of her reserves to stand up straight. He swayed a little under the motion, and almost pulled both of them back down, but she counter-balanced and took a calming breath before moving again. Using the same method she had used to carry the young livestock as a child, she put her head down and moved onward. She let herself fall forward a little with each step, her strong leg muscles stopping the fall each time, and keeping the movement flowing in the direction she was facing. If they were attacked now, she would be unable to defend herself or the elder, but she pushed the thought away. There was nothing else to do now except walk on one step at a time, and that was all she allowed her mind to dwell on. There were no sounds behind her. Taroo was silent, his breathing shallow, and the forest further behind him offered no more surprises for the time being.

It took her much longer to get to the tree than she thought it would. The ground was rockier on foot than she remembered, and the horses had made it seem easy.

She lay the old man down in a cluster of thick branches at the fallen tree's base, and took a moment to re-consider her possible actions. Grey Wolf's breathing was regular and strong, so she guessed he was in no immediate danger. She could either try to awaken Taroo or stay and guard the elder. She decided that the risk of leaving the old man was worth gaining an extra pair of hands to help her. She covered the old man as best as she could with the foliage and raced back toward the attack site.

Old Grey Wolf was alone again. He opened his eyes and exhaled, wincing as he pushed himself to his feet. Checking that Akuti had not returned or changed her mind, he waited a few moments before walking away from the safety of the path, and deeper into the forest.

FORTY-THREE

Young President Freeman stared into the polished aluminum wall mirror. His beard was longer than he usually liked it, but high security military wings for delusional national security risks were not the best places for razor blades it seemed. He wheeled back into position at the window. It was dark outside now and he could hear the other inmates settling down for the night. This usually involved screaming and shouting and general high decibel activities, rather than the expected opposite. Freeman supposed it made sense, given the nature of his accommodation. He heard footsteps as his own personal butler came to tuck him in for the night.

Showtime.

The orderly was in good spirits and had a pair of white earphones dangling from inside his collar. Tinned music spilled out of them.

"How are we tonight? Any flying robots with us this evening?"

Freeman remained silent and distant as usual as the orderly went about his evening routine. Freeman had been force-feeding them nothing but silence for weeks now, getting them accustomed to his long bouts of absolute compliance and docile nature. He wasn't sure if it had been long enough yet, but he guessed it was as convincing as it was going to get. They had seen him do nothing more spectacular than drool for almost forty-five days, and he had faked the need for help to eat, drink and urinate for his entire stay. He had forced himself to lose his balance on a couple of occasions, even spilling himself helplessly onto the ground at one time as two orderlies had tried to help him into bed. The overall effect wasn't entirely what he hoped, but it was still enough. They were still cautious around him, and still almost borderline professional. This was the military after all. Professionalism and effectiveness were habitual and bad habits were difficult to fall into here. But a couple of the orderlies had become almost comfortable around him. And that was how he needed them.

It needed a certain type of individual to deviate from the set routines in an establishment where the most effective way to do things was programmed into the routine from day one. The individual in question would have to be happy enough in his job to want to do it correctly and to the letter, but would need an air of arrogance that would let his own judgment cloud his ability to recall his training, for only a moment. And he'd have to be tired and alone.

Freeman had studied the patterns of the orderlies' shifts meticulously over the course of the past few weeks. He knew that the morning shifts worked regular hours and were always the same team. The afternoon and late shifts were pooled from a different group of staff, but also included some of the morning crew, looking to do some overtime. Every once in a while, a morning crew member would clock off in the early afternoon, and would return in the evening. His partner on duty would do the same, but for some reason would not do so until later on. Not until *after* the evening room change. Freeman guessed it was either cutbacks or shortages, and while it only meant an hour or so of being understaffed, Freeman had identified it as a weakness. This only happened every eleven days. It had happened on Freeman's first day there, and it had also happened on the forty-fourth day. Which was today. It was an essential part of his escape plan. Which was why it had to be today. If he didn't he would have to wait another eleven days. He was done talking to apparitions, and he was done drooling down his own damned chin.

The nurse was called Brian. At least that's what it said on his shirt collar. Freeman let him complete most of his routine. He watched in the window's reflection as Brian cleaned out the supper tray behind him. Watched him fold down the stiff sheets on the steel bed, and plump up the pillow. Brian whistled as he did so, and Freeman almost felt bad for Brian.

Almost.

Brian carried the tray toward the door, placed it on the floor and came around the other side of the bed to retrieve the bedpan from the foot of the bed, where he'd left it that afternoon. When he couldn't see it he scooted around until he was between Freeman and the bed and bent down to look under the bed. He never stood back up. Freeman hit him hard on the back of the head with the steel pan. Brian's head gave a little with the force of the blow, and he slumped face first into the bed, before tumbling less than elegantly onto the floor. The bed shifted a little under the weight, but it made no more noise than Brian's wheezing breaths did. Freeman listened carefully for any irregularities outside his room, but heard nothing from the hallway that indicated any reinforcements were coming. Only the canned music coming from the earphones broke the natural silence. Freeman acted quickly and stole the orderly's belt and security card. Then he wheeled himself toward the door, before swiping the lock open.

Once he was outside the door he would be on any number of security monitors. Which is why he wouldn't be leaving through the door. Reaching around the open gap with the belt buckle, he blindly felt around for the doorjamb on the opposite side. He wasn't overly worried about being seen. In this light, any small objects making minimal movements would hardly register on a monitor. Anything that was less than human sized was generally ignored on security screens. It was just a fact of life.

Freeman clipped the buckle in pace and pulled the door closed, fighting against the door's automatic closing motor. When the door was flush with the frame he swiped the card again and yanked the belt as hard as he could. The door lock light turned amber, before flashing red intermittently, and the door bolted closed in three separate locations along the frame. Freeman guessed a silent alarm was now warning everyone on the site that an inmate was trying to use a key card inappropriately and that the automatic door had been forced shut manually from the outside to prevent this happening.

Freeman wheeled himself back to Brian and relieved him of his earphones and music player.

Moving himself to the center of the room, he used the headphones to gently swing the mp3 player in an arc, generating enough momentum to gradually spin it in a widening circular motion without exerting so much force that it detached itself from its weak connection to the headphone jack. Satisfied that the object was on a semi-consistent orbit around his wrist, Freeman used all of the strength in his legs to simultaneously stand up as straight as he could, and reach as high as he could with his swinging arm. The music player's path remained in its constant orbital trajectory, but the entire pathway was now displaced vertically, which brought the mp3 player into direct contact with the room's military-efficient, no-fuss singular light bulb. A hollow deep pop as the bulb's vacuum quickly de-pressurized, and the total darkness, told Freeman that his aim was better than he hoped. Slumping back down into his chair he slowed the arc quickly into a controlled fall onto his lap. He fought past the burning pain from his acrobatics. The little amount of physiotherapy he'd been able to practice under the cover of darkness each night had helped a little, but he was now running on adrenalin alone and he would have to be quick.

He pulled himself from the chair and into a seating position on the bed. He took off his standard grey issue t-shirt and with more than a little difficulty, managed to haul the orderly out of his white jacket. He balled this under his pillow out of sight, and re-dressed Brian clumsily in his own sweat soaked shirt instead. Now came the fun part. Using the chair for leverage, Freeman half dragged, half lifted Brian into a semblance of a seating position in the wheel chair and pushed him away from the bed and toward the window. Then, he crawled as fast as he could under the bed.

Benjamin Freeman then waited for his chance to make the perfect escape.

FORTY-FOUR

The General seemed distant. He was toying with a prosthetic limb of one of the technicians. Its base was charred from the events at the lab.

Freeman chuckled at him and shook his head.

"Still sentimental as ever I see."

The General looked up, smiling. "Just wondering how the hell we pulled off that pantomime in there. Any one little deviation could have killed any one of us."

"But it didn't."

"And it didn't because it couldn't? Or because it just didn't this time?" the General rubbed his eyes. He couldn't remember when he last saw his personal quarters. "This timeline stuff is enough to bend you right the way up to crazy."

"I won't argue with that," said Freeman. "It's just that when you've seen it from my perspective, you get a little blasé about the how and the why of it. Too busy actually dealing with it to ponder about it. I guess that's a luxury I'll leave to you lab-rats."

Behind Freeman, stacked three shelves high, were various artificial body parts. All of which were surplus stock from the war effort. Decoys. During the end of the uprising they had used the synthetics' technology against them and staged large civilian retreats using decoy bots. Unlike synths the bots only had a single processing unit and couldn't think outside its pre-programmed operating window. They were robots only by primitive definition. They could behave and act like both humans and synthetics, but were no more advanced than the software written and stored within them.

"I can't believe I fell for it. All of those years ago. And today of course. Such a strange thing to see that moment in my life again as an outsider." Freeman lowered his head as his mind drifted.

"Do you wish it could be different?" the General asked.

Freeman smiled. "Every day. Every damned day."

The intercom buzzed. "General Daniels. There's a call for you. She says its urgent. She won't leave her name."

Daniels trotted to the nearest line and patched the call through. "Daniels here. How can I help?"

Freeman watched with curiosity as the General's face became worried and then visibly paler. He placed his hand over the receiver and spoke directly to the old man.

"It's Jack. He's dead."

FORTY-FIVE

Freeman closed his eyes and tried to breathe regularly. This was difficult to do because two orderlies were pounding at the door with what he guessed was a fire-axe. It was almost time. He wasn't sure if he was strong enough yet, but he had a feeling that this was his best chance to make this work. He only needed to get past the furthest patrol path and the trees at the end of the security fence. If he could get behind the cover of those trees then he'd have a chance.

The room was dark. From his spot under the bed, Freeman could see Brian the nurse's silhouette perfectly framed in the moonlight. Brian was breathing heavily, and would be for a while, guessing from the sound the bedpan had made on his skull. Freeman took the longest shard of the splintered light bulb and clenched his teeth. He scratched a long line down his left arm, on the upper side. He didn't want to risk cutting a vein. The blood trickled down gradually and freeman counted the drops as they pooled into his open right hand. When he counted six drops he licked his palm, making sure to get all of it at the same time.

His mind was instantly hazy and his body became a warm, safe place. Then he was violently snatched out of it and was suddenly falling through a terrible darkness.

The orderlies saw none of this and carried on their brutal attack of the steel door, stopping only to check momentarily through the thick square of glass that their prisoner had not moved from his position by the window.

FORTY-SIX

Rogers had walked for most of the morning and had found no trace of the book. The tracks had quickly dried up and he'd best-guessed his way from there, but he was no woodsman, and now he had a feeling that he might also be lost. The sun was high in the sky and filtered through only when the majestic conifers thinned out. He had the world's meanest hangover, despite being sure he'd had no more than his usual, and his sneakers were no good against the terrain. Rogers had had enough. He slumped to his knees at the base of a splintered tree and took a minute to gather his thoughts. He pushed most of his worries away and tried to categorize the most pressing matters. His wife had left him, he's had some sort of mental breakdown, he had lost the most important item he owned, and he was lost in the woods. He vaguely remembered speaking to his foster father, but it danced away from him when he tried to think any more about it. His head felt like a buzz saw's playground.

If only he could remember how the hell he'd gotten here. He had a feeling that his memory was getting fuzzier instead of clearer as the day went on. It was how his hangovers usually worked; he was just a little concerned that this was more than that. As he sat, catching his breath, the gurgling and splashes of running water caught his attention. His fractured mind dragged the background noise back into focus and he pushed himself up and walked toward it. Water was a good thing. He guessed he was more than a little dehydrated, and fixing that would surely help make at least some of his problems disappear.

The sound grew clearer as he walked up the incline, and suddenly he was standing in bright sunlight, with a mountain stream twinkling and splashing down into a natural rock pool. Rogers made his way carefully to the water's edge, and drank eagerly from his cupped hands. The water was cold and biting, and he was surprised how soft it felt compared to his faucet at home.

Home. When would he ever get home? This was ridiculous. He was a city cop, and too old to be lost in the woods like a runaway school kid. *If it wasn't for that damned book.*

This last thought was stopped abruptly, because his eyes had wandered with his train of thoughts. He had been scanning the vegetation and the running water, and the contrast between the light near the pool and the shadows only a foot or two past the tree line. It was somewhere between the two that the old man was sitting, holding a gun and a book. Rogers' breath caught in his throat and he rose slowly to his feet, never taking his eyes off the old man. It wasn't the fact that the man was armed or that he seemed to be holding his book. He couldn't take his eyes off the man because he was dressed in full native American regalia that looked about as authentic as you could get, and from the way the shadows played across the scene from this angle, it looked to Rogers just like the man had two faces.

FORTY-SEVEN

The double doors slid open silently, and the two men pushed in. Freeman went first, his chair clacking across the grill as the floor changed from rubber to sterile steel. General Daniels, his head bowed, followed behind, leaning against his old friend's chair as he walked. They passed a wall of cylindrical cubicles, each one the size and shape of a man.

"It's amazing isn't it?" Freeman paused. His chair clicked and whirred to a stop. "All of these advances in our knowledge, everything we've done, all that we have become. And we still can't cure a damned cold." He glanced up at the pods, taking his eyes away from Daniels. Each pod was numbered, the numbers here at the end of the line reaching one thousand, and Daniels had personally installed all of them. *So many years of work, and for what?* Freeman placed a hand on the closest, feeling the hum of life bubbling behind the glass.

"These were going to change everything. Make sure we were back on the right track. Humanity. The funny thing is, I can't remember what it means to be part of it. You and Jack are all the species I have left..." Freeman's voice cracked "*had* left."

Daniels shook his head, and looked down the corridor. The pods stretched into the darkness as far as he could see, blinking and pulsing with their own lives inside. "Let's get this over with. Talking about it isn't going to bring him back. Nothing's changed. We still have our fallback." Freeman nodded quietly, his eyes wet and tired. He moved the chair on, away from the cocoons, aiming toward a discreet brushed steel door, standing between two banks of processors. Daniels positioned himself slightly ahead of Freeman and reached up above the doorframe. His fingers felt along the shallow rim until they brushed against and almost dislodged the object sitting there. It was an old brass key, probably the last of its kind. Daniels unlocked the door. Freeman moved into the gloom, and Daniels followed, closing the door behind him.

The lights took a moment to come on. Then they blinked on twice very briefly, giving them a snapshot of the scene before plunging the place into darkness again, then a click and a ping, and the room was illuminated with natural looking light. On the far side of the small room, a single bed was bolted to the wall, and a man's shape lay beneath the covers. A glass panel joined the room to what looked like an office space next door, and a visibly distressed orderly held up a shaky hand in greeting. She offered half a smile in condolence and walked out, leaving them to their business.

The room seemed colder than usual, and the life support machines embedded in the walls were silent.

Freeman wheeled himself closer to the unit's only bed, and the General matched the pace quietly alongside him. They had been here many times over the years, yet this was a new experience for both of them. They had come to say their final goodbyes to this room. The old man reached a hand out onto the soft medical linen and gazed at the man in the bed.

Jack. No words were spoken, and none were needed. The old man in the bed was gone now. Freeman looked at Jack's face, and saw something of himself there. *How did we ever get so damned old?* Life had been a blink of the eye. Freeman quietly wheeled himself back around and away from the bed, and stopped only to wait for the doors to slide open. General Daniels watched him leave and gathered his own thoughts. Today things would change. The General wondered how this would affect Freeman's health. How much more did the old soldier have left in him? Daniels placed a final goodbye touch on Jack's arm and left the room with purpose. There was work to be done, and now more than ever, not a single second to waste.

EPILOGUE

The medical orderly, having composed herself, walked back into the room to get the package she had left behind. The old man had only three items to his name, which had been zipped up in a clear airtight container; a wooden coin, a writing implement and a battered dark brown journal. The once-hard cover of the book had softened with years of use and ugly dark blotches only hinted at the book's original condition. The spine had all but disintegrated. The inside flap, however, revealed that the sun-bleached cover used to be a magnificent deep black.

Made in the USA
San Bernardino, CA
11 April 2017